# BY THEIR COLD FINGERS

By

Timothy Bryan

*"If you grumble when you are ill, then God will not grant you death."*

**- Platon Karataev, Lev Tolstoy's *War and Peace***

# Table of Contents

# Chapter One

## Eastern Settlement, Greenland. 1408 AD

The early afternoon sun was barely visible across the bleak landscape, with roiling clouds blotting out the few rays of light spreading from the southeastern sky. Wind howled across this remote area, speaking with icy breath to a forbidding and remote background of snow-covered mountain peaks hovering on the distant horizon.

Set between discolored rocks and sparse clusters of cold-resistant foliage, a gentle river wound its way from those distant mountains, working its way into the vast ocean that spanned west. Where the fresh water merged with the dark oceanic tides was calm, with only a few ripples from the colliding waters showing any separation in their newly merged paths.

The confluence of the river and sea was surrounded by stone-covered beaches, where the rocks were an odd combination of ancient dark bedrock and water-worn pebbles swept over time from distant glaciers in the uninhabited interior of Greenland.

Huddling against the cold breeze and colder water stood two men. Dressed in simple peasant clothing, they waded in the river, grunting and pulling on a crude net stretched across the lapping river current. On the shore, their exterior cloaks and animal skins were piled on a tattered blanket.

Farther from the water's edge was a modest campfire, which crackled alongside a donkey attached to a simple cart. The animal stared at the two men with indifferent eyes, looking rather bored as it evaluated their exertions.

Kristian righted himself in the calm tide as he struggled with the sinewy net barrier. He ignored the shivers that racked his body while he grasped the edge of their underwater fishing snare.

Collecting his strength, Kristian yanked on the crude handmade net. In his early twenties, he had an innocent quality to him, which wasn't the sort of thing expected of people living on the edge of civilization. Bashful and full of self-doubt, he lowered his face, as if the fishing problems could only be caused by his own incompetence.

"Never felt something so heavy," Kristian said, trying to avoid complaining. "Feels like it's caught on a striped whale."

Shaking his head, his father Erik waded farther into the shallow river, where he struggled with the task of helping his son. Well into middle age, Erik's skin was as weathered as a dried fish, and whatever youth he possessed was in his lithe muscular frame, not the deep lines of his too-early-aged face. He shrugged as he yanked harder on the stuck net.

Raising his voice, Erik gestured for them to pull at the same time. His face was determined, but his demeanor was understanding and pleasant. "Your mother, rest her soul, will avoid meeting me in the afterlife if I raise a weakling, so pull…HARDER."

Straining from the effort, Erik lost his balance and splashed into the dark water. His head disappeared briefly, and when he reemerged, he could barely catch his breath from the frigid shock. He spent several moments regaining his bearing while Kristian gazed worriedly over at him.

Chagrined, Erik finally was able to speak through his sharp-drawn breaths. "Well, that wasn't graceful."

Erik and Kristian met eyes and burst out laughing, enjoying a hearty chuckle from the pathetic state of their fishing expedition. Their snickers carried on even as the to-the-bone cold made their laughs come in rhythm with their incessantly cold shakes.

The surge of humility and humor allowed Erik to warm up a bit, but he pointed to the shore in a bid for self-preservation from hypothermia. Licking at his lips, he tried to avoid going numb from the intense cold. "I'm gonna dry off—before I freeze to death."

Kristian stepped out of Erik's way as his father stumbled across the rocky bottom on the way to the shoreline. Making for the deeper part of the gentle water, Kristian huffed in determination. "It must be stuck on some rocks. I'll free it up."

Looking back from the shoreline, Erik threw a fluffy bearskin hide on his shoulders to warm himself. Grimacing from the chill, Erik watched his son reach below the surface of the river.

Kristian's eyes were confused as he felt around in the murky shallows. He concentrated as he pawed through the net, feeling for the source of their troubles. His smile faded as he grasped something in his half-frozen fingers, his expression growing more perplexed as his digits worked their way around a huge stuck object.

With a celebratory grunt, Kristian yanked free a dead arctic char, holding it up above his head in a celebratory thrust. His features were elated as he stared over at his surprised father. "There's a bunch of them caught in the net. Wonder what made 'em collect in the middle there? Never seen so many in one place."

Peering at the fish trophy, Erik was as happy as he was surprised. He grinned the grin of a celebratory boy, and the wrinkles on his creased face made the smile endearing, even with several gaps in his poor teeth. "Ha. We'll eat for a month. I knew our luck would change."

Casting aside his warm blanket, Erik grinned as he waded back into the freezing waterway. Struggling next to his son, he enthusiastically plunged his own hands below the icy surface.

#

Erik dropped another of the slick chars on the growing pile of shiny fish. The area around their camp was covered with their precious haul, as if the earth itself birthed the catch of delectable seafood. Both father and son grinned widely, knowing they had struck gold for their fishing efforts.

Erik was particularly pleased with their fish-harvesting luck. He had lived on this frozen frontier long enough to know when a good bounty is at hand. Every year the water got colder, and the floating ice in the nearby fjords grew ever thicker. Making a living and having sufficient stores of food required a man to grab what was available when it pops up, and he would make sure to use every calorie from the gaggle of fish lying on the shoreline.

Falling on his ass next to Kristian, Erik breathed deep from the extended work. He threw a cloak over his legs as he propped his feet near the campfire, wiggling his toes to reclaim feeling in them. As he took in the clean air, the pace of his breaths fell off, making his contented expression into a dreamy stare. He peered over the deserted ocean to their side. "Never seen anything like it. Glad we came out today, it'll take your mind off…"

Erik's voice drifted off as he stopped that train of thought. Sometimes, he didn't know when to shut his own mouth, even for an old fool like himself—a man who should have damn well known better.

Kristian lowered his eyes from the barren surroundings, losing the relaxed smile that had been making itself home on his face. He sulked as he ran a pair of rocks over in his fingers, clacking them softly together.

Erik nodded an apology, hoping to salvage the good mood. "I'm sorry about Sigri, son, but she has to do what's best for her family. And…the village. It's how the world works. It isn't fair, like everything else that happens in life, but it's part of the bargain we have with the Good Lord."

"The Good Lord?" replied Kristian, and he looked over to Erik with doubtful eyes. "He wants me to be alone and unhappy? Losing the only thing that ever mattered to me?"

Erik took a while to answer, mulling over the innocence and blind idealism of youth. He knew it was part of growing up, but that didn't make overcoming life's disappointments and heartbreaks any easier. "No, the bargain is we do our best, in the very limited time we have—no matter what we face."

Kristian didn't answer. Instead, he merely focused on the crackling fire.

Sighing, Erik tried another approach, hoping to depersonalize his son's broken heart. "You've seen the Bishop's residence at Gardar, back when we actually had a bishop? The one with the big tower that used to hold that huge church bell?"

Looking confused, Kristian nodded, unsure of where this was going.

"And you've seen that fancy graveyard, the one with all the important people who've ever lived in this country. They got beautiful crosses above their long-dead bodies, even though the deepening grass or ice covers their plots most of the year."

Kristian tilted his head, still unsure but staring with sudden interest at Erik.

Erik continued, meeting his son's gaze with warmth and understanding. "Every one of those people from hundreds of years ago had troubles, loss, fear…and heartbreak. It's what life is, along with occasional moments of joy—like you had with Sigri. To focus on the bad instead of the good is to let the happiness mean nothing."

Shuffling his feet together, Erik stood and stretched. Holding his fingers over the heat of the campfire, he tried his best voice of wisdom. "Because in the end, the few decades we get here will be replaced by eternity with God. And, I bet we won't be focusing on the bad when we're there."

This got an uncertain grin from Kristian, who pondered Erik's words with detached eyes.

"Well, you get the net," said Erik, gesturing to the river and changing the subject. "I'll clean the fish, and we'll be home before dark. Getting too damn cold at night—every year it gets worse."

As Erik pulled out a sharp knife to clean the fish, Kristian nodded and stumbled to the water, extending his legs with each stride to get the cramps out of his muscles.

It took Kristian some time to pull the net in as he rearranged the twisted-hide rope into an orderly pile after collecting it from the cold water. When he got to the end of the coiled rope, his confused eyes locked on something caught in the last bit of frayed line.

Reaching down, he pulled on a whitish string, disentangling it from the rope. His gaze moved into the shallows, where the material extended into the water.

Kristian's mouth hung open, and he pointed into the river. "F…father?"

Looking up from a pile of fish, Erik glanced to where his son was pointing. "What's wrong?"

Still holding a gutted fish, Erik walked to the edge of the shore, stopping at his son's side. They both stared out, shocked and unsure of what they were seeing.

In the water, a bloated corpse of a man floated. Dressed in dark priestly vestments, his abdomen was exposed and sliced open, and his chest cavity was inundated with glistening water. His pale face had an open mouth with blue lips, while his clouded dead eyes stared to the side, like he didn't wish to make eye contact with his discoverers. Loops of his intestines drifted in the lazy current, and Kristian held the end of those innards where it was caught in the net.

Several fish swam around the dead man, nibbling at various portions of his rotting flesh. There seemed to be a never-ending supply of swimming char seeking to enjoy a last meal from the helpless corpse.

A disgusted expression crossed Erik's face, and he dropped his half-cleaned fish onto the rocks as he took a deep breath. *So much for our good luck.*

# Chapter Two

The gorgeous Hvalsey Church sat on an open field surrounded by half-frozen pastures full of rocks and stunted trees. The building was constructed of form-fitted stones aligned to perfection, with a wide-doored entryway at its main steps and numerous stained-glass windows facing from either of its long sides. The exterior was mortared with an orderly white sheen, making the building visible from long distances due to its almost-glowing chalky color.

In the nearby meadows, splinted rails of long-disused fences encompassed the tawdry fields, and a few cattle foraged on what little grass was available. It was a picture of an attractive but declining parish, one that was low on investment and caretakers.

A peaceful but long-worn graveyard was located to the side of the structure. Various stained headstones and worn wooden crosses of long-dead parishioners appeared rather sad in the afternoon light, providing a somber ambiance to the isolated house of worship. The local priest's diminutive house stood behind the cemetery, its simple stone walls looking decidedly plain in comparison to the attractive church.

The church stood on a rise above the ocean, and the sea below spanned toward the horizon, its white-capped waves announcing rough water conditions far into the distance. The alluring but dangerous ocean was as captivating as it was lonely, and numerous icebergs huddled in the water as they drifted south on the strong currents of the arctic as they floated into the North Atlantic Ocean.

Inside the building, lively medieval music played, offering a lyrical and pleasant backdrop to crowds of revelers. The cross of the crucified Jesus stood against a far wall, surrounded by murals of the saints and the Virgin Mary. The aged paintings seemed to gaze down approvingly at the crowds, as if they were happy to witness the festive occasion.

Peasants filled the church to the brim, and smiles and loud banter accompanied a mood of enthusiastic celebration. Their clothing and bearing were modest, but it was an environment of believers, with hopeful expressions of joy throughout the large and warm room.

Several musicians sat to the side of the teeming mass, plying their lutes and harps with practiced expertise as they continued their lively serenade.

Attendants wove throughout the chattering groups, offering drinks and treats to the onlookers. The eager faces of the celebrants were universally flushed by shared body heat, and with each passing moment, the sound of boisterous conversations forced the auditory level higher.

In the corner of the cheery fracas stood a pretty woman dressed in an attractive wedding gown. Smiling sheepishly, she nodded thanks to passing well-wishers. Sigri, just out of her teens and fitted with diligently applied makeup, was the center of all this attention, but appeared uncomfortable with the fuss of the wedding reception. She glanced nervously to the side, searching for a pair of friendly eyes.

Rand met her gaze with a determined and fatherly nod. In his fifties, his clothing exuded the appearance of one who aspired to the upper crest of society, but who fell short of the funds to quite make it happen.

Standing across from father and daughter was a smiling man, Thorstein, and in his case, there could be no doubt of his wealth and pedigree. His colorful robe and brimless black hat would have made him at ease in any royal setting, but in this rural environment, he stuck out like a well-groomed thumb. He was but a few years younger than Rand, but a pampered life left his face less marred by wrinkles, and his smile was otherwise covered under an aristocratic goatee.

Thorstein's adoring gaze focused on Sigri for a moment, and he spoke to Rand while holding her stare. "Are you not satisfied with the amount? It is as we…agreed."

Rand kept a respectful tone, even as he nodded doubtfully. "The amount isn't the issue. The estate in Reykjavik is more than generous. Our…family has lived in Greenland for hundreds of years."

Rand lowered his voice, taking great care to ensure he wasn't overheard. "You promised to consider making your home HERE."

Thorstein tilted his head to Rand, speaking in a moderate tone. It was the tone of a businessman, one who never revealed his objective—unless that was his intent. "I am considering it, as I promised. But that doesn't equate to a promise to settle here."

Sigri scowled, looking mildly annoyed with Thorstein, but he managed to remain calm under her disapproving glare. Smiling meekly, Thorstein held his hand out to Sigri, which she reluctantly took in her own. She focused on her new husband, watching his every word and expression.

"My family's wealth and prestige are centered in Iceland," Thorstein explained, pausing as he found the right words to continue. "Bringing you and your daughter into our good name requires my assets from there, correct?"

Rand grimaced as he considered the explanation. "Yes, but how do we remain here when your property and assets are eight hundred miles across the ocean? More ships are lost every year to the seas, making travel for my daughter disproportionately dangerous."

Thorstein sighed, conceding the point with a frown. "People have been fleeing Greenland for generations. This land grows difficult to farm and livestock dies off. The population decreases every year."

Rand took a step forward. He put a pleading hand on Thorstein's arm, which got a surprised look from both Thorstein and Sigri. "You're a merchant, Thorstein. You've made a fortune trading with us. When times are difficult, the price is lowest. You can buy up most of the land for a few crowns—."

From the altar, Father Galmand cleared his throat. Deep into middle age, the jowly and bearded priest scanned his flock carefully. With caring eyes and a robust frame, he was the embodiment of a doting pastor.

Rand stepped back from Thorstein as the low roar of the crowd and the music died away. He wasn't pleased, but he fell silent as he peered up at the priest. He was a man that knew when to argue and when to keep his mouth shut. So, he opted to fight another day, or to at least make his case in a better and more private environment.

Galmand smoothed over his vestments in preparation for a speech, while the expectant villagers waited in silence. "Today, we have witnessed the joining of two souls in holy matrimony," said Galmand, and he scanned the crowd, gauging the effect of each of his words on their upbeat faces. "Two of God's children—who were meant for one another."

At the mention of their lives being fated for each other, Sigri glanced around uncomfortably. Large discrepancies in age among married couples were not uncommon in the village, but a union with an outsider was far from a conventional occurrence.

Thorstein noticed her apprehension, and his enthusiastic features wilted into a frown.

Galmand fussed with his unrumpled priestly garments, running his pudgy fingers across the silken purple cloth. The nervous habit lent a sense of considered reflection to his words as he puffed out his chest. "But it is not to God alone that we praise such a bond between two of his followers. No, our Father in heaven enables such a match, so that we can celebrate as a community…celebrate a bond that can reinvigorate our faithful people."

Now, it was Thorstein that glanced around awkwardly, adopting his own nervous habit of running his hand over the clean-shaven, nonexistent stubble on his face. Both Sigri and Rand noticed the evasive gesture, but Rand in particular focused on him with a biting stare.

"Our faith is strengthened by this new marriage, in the belief that we can welcome new blood into our town," continued Galmand. "And…see a future of prosperity, at a time when there is so much worry amongst God's children."

As one, the entirety of the church's congregants focused on Thorstein, their smiles punctuated by respect and admiration. For a moment, he was the only person of interest in the sweaty confines of the communal area. Thorstein blushed under the fusillade of stares, suddenly appearing like he wanted to be somewhere else entirely.

After the pregnant silence passed, Galmand clapped his hands together, then held them up in a show of religious exhortation. "Remember, the Lord helps those that help themselves. We are not merely to act on faith, but to embrace changes in our lives to ensure beneficial individual outcomes, as well as those of our neighbors. Now, let us celebrate this new marriage as we accept Thorstein Olafsson into our community. It is a time of great joy."

Galmand motioned for the party to recommence, and the music started anew. The crowds restarted their personal conversations and refocused away from the newly wedded couple. All was well in the pleasant and lighthearted atmosphere, with smiling faces and happy thoughts flowing in abundance.

Thorstein and Sigri glanced nervously at one another, each for their own reasons.

#

Outside the church, the limited light of the waning day illuminated the wedding party as they gathered into a milling crowd. They were spread out in the back of the cemetery, groups of villagers staring in quiet and rapt attention. The crowds' eyes fixed on a long sandpit, where at each end of the groomed earth, a metal rod stuck up from the ground.

Staring with almost maniacal concentration, Rand stood at one end, his lips pursed in anticipation. Stepping up, he lofted underhand a round-iron piece of metal. The object careened through the late-afternoon light, where it clanked around the metal rod at the far end in a ringing bulls-eye. It was a perfect throw in the medieval game of Quoits, similar to horseshoes and a mainstay in entertainment for outdoor enjoyment.

The crowd around him erupted in applause, and Rand pumped his fist in victory at the impressive feat. Behind him, Thorstein covered his smiling face with one hand, chagrined at being bested by the local favorite. Standing by her husband's side, Sigri clapped with a wide grin, proud of her father's skillful exploit. Her smile grew into a gloating leer as she nudged Thorstein with her elbow, making sure to wink at her humbled partner.

#

Some time later, Galmand stood with Rand, Thorstein, and some of the local residents, grinning into a raging campfire that had been built to offer outside heat for the all-day wedding celebration. Most of the people in attendance had already left for home, doddering off toward their homesteads on the dirt track near the church, but a significant portion remained to enjoy the relaxing community event as it wound down. In the background, a few rays of the sun's remaining light painted the clouded sky an attractive hue of orange.

The swoosh of sturdy waves from the nearby beach added a substantial and raucous backdrop to the party, making it seem less isolated for the moment. Sometimes, the sound of the outdoors could be comforting and reduce loneliness, while at others, the raw wildness of the natural world produced the opposite effect at such a distant outpost of humanity.

In the earlier past, when a few hundred Viking Icelanders came to colonize these uninhabited shores, it must have seemed like another world to those settlers, a place where only the endless frothy waves and seabirds would offer consoling company from the ravages of the unknown frontier. But since that distant time, with centuries of Norse habitation altering the landscape, it was like the rural environment itself was as much a friend to the settlers as the next farm's residents in this sparsely populated region.

One of the female attendants to the party held a tray of baked rolls out to Rand and Galmand. Thorstein shook his head in polite refusal to the offer, but to his side, Galmand eagerly accepted two of the sweetened baked treats. As the young server nodded and moved on, Galmand stopped her again to get one last helping of the delectable breads, and he was barely able to balance the varied food in his pudgy hands as he considered which to eat first.

Farther away from the fire, a group of young women stood in a circle with Sigri. The bride beamed in the firelight, chatting with her excited face lit up and enjoying the attention as something of a local celebrity. Her gathered friends peered over at Thorstein, their eyes locked in unhidden envy at her betrothal to her rich and handsome husband.

Rand noticed the attention and admiration of the locals for Sigri, and he beamed with pride as his gaze moved back to his daughter. His focus was not just that of a proud father, but also of a man who was glad to elevate his position in the community.

His ego was attached to his happiness for his daughter, making her future a reflection of his own hopes and dreams.

Sigri noticed her father's pretension and wasn't enamored with the interaction, as well as the accompanying politics of this village she had grown up in. She wasn't ashamed at the chance to vault her way ahead in the local social strata; life was too short to avoid the possibilities that marrying up could give a young lady. But still, she had always seen herself as the champion for her people and their way of life, however humble it was. To be the only local to land the affection of a rich merchant was impressive, but it was also kind of sad, like she had left the village's less fortunate behind.

Thinking harder, Sigri realized it must have been the same in all those far-off capitals of Europe she had read about in Thorstein's extensive library. Hordes of poor people lived in squalor throughout those distant, huge cities such as Paris, but on occasion, some of them must also have struck it rich through some wedded arrangement. At least here, she would have preferred to remain in both worlds, with poor friends and rich new acquaintances alike to keep her company. That way, the boost in social status could also have been accompanied by her heartfelt attachment to her former life and people.

Sigri's smile faded a bit, and she sighed as she returned her gaze to the firelight. With an unsettled frown, she castigated herself for getting too hung up on the past. *Forge ahead, but remember where you came from.*

#

The remains of receding daytime had subsumed into pale early night. It was still early in terms of customary sleep patterns, but being Fall at this far northern latitude meant that darkness came early, increasing the perpetual chill of the oncoming cold season.

All but a handful of guests had departed the area, but what was left were having a final happy jaunt in the lively celebration, hosting big grins on their faces after the fatiguing party. The musicians moved their activities around the fire, sitting on stumps and playing their instruments with boisterous grins in the shadows of the encroaching darkness. For the moment, their played tunes blunted the nighttime, offering respite from encroaching cold and the seclusion of the rural church.

Groups of dancers held each other's arms in the scant illumination of the fire, hopping to the spirited tunes in clumsy appreciation of the moment. In a circle around the couples, clapping friends serenaded their movements with jovial precision, snapping their hands together with the rhythm of the joyous music.

For the moment, this world was a pleasant place of happiness and neighborly appreciation. Thorstein and Sigri hopped at the center of the enthusiastic crowd, swinging each other with unabashed smiles and enjoying the final moments of their wedding celebration.

#

The remote mountain peaks were colored a dark and forbidding black, with sharp outlines shrouded in misty clouds and interspersed with layers of jagged ice. Weathered rock spires ran the length of the extended mountain range, looking like the spine of some horrid monster jutting up at irregular intervals across the height of Greenland's desolate interior. Its raw slabs of snow and cracked stone stretched for hundreds of miles into light-starved skies on the distant outlines of the horizon.

Even for this vast continent-sized island, where only a few hardy souls dared to carve out a living, this was inaccessible and savage territory. With cliffs and ice shelves that never witnessed the footprints of man or beast, it was perfect in its raw and frightening nature, devoid of life or inclination to ever be tamed.

In the midst of this impossibly remote area, on a particularly sheer cliff face, the barely defined hole of a cave faced the shrieking wind of a far northern gale. Within the orifice, a faint red light emanated, blinking from deep inside as its intensity pulsed with a dull hum.

From the cave opening, a natural passageway ran deep into the mountainside, twisting amongst jagged passageways towards the mountain core. Far in that ragged corridor, the dull light grew brighter, humming with a bizarre sound, a sound that could only be defined as disturbing and otherworldly. The unnatural moans of unrealized screams portended a frightful and wicked destination, with faint and inhuman wails lying at the edge of human understanding.

The twisting passage ended in an enormous cavern, where the shrieking sound was constant and louder, seeming to emanate from the reddish stone of the strange rock walls themselves. The ancient surfaces of the interior formations glowed with the pitch of that odd tormented sound, lighting the surrounding area of stalactites and hewn pathways with its pulsating light. The wide cave area around was filled with boulders and broken rock deposits, their slick surfaces glowing under the abnormal light.

A figure emerged from an opening to the back of the cave, its dark outline striding toward the center of the vast enclosure. In the center of the cavern was a fire, its flames licking from beneath a large cauldron. The container contained a bubbling dark liquid, but its odd shape didn't appear to be metal; instead, it seemed to be made of the same substance as the pulsing walls enclosing the entire area, as if the stones themselves were fashioned into the receptacle by some bizarre and powerful force.

The hiss of the bubbling fluid accentuated the raw, tortured voices resounding from the hellish walls. The Keelut approached the strange vessel, stopping in front of the flames and looking into the hissing fluid.

The creature was tall and lithe, with blue-whitish flesh running the length of its bizarre frame. Its head was elongated, with slits for a nose and a black mouth filled with incisor teeth. Straight black lips surrounded the sharp teeth and no emotion covered its emotionless face. No ears were evident on the sides of its head, and no hair was visible across its white-translucent exterior.

The being was naked but had no genitals or obvious means of reproduction. Its body appeared to glow as if it had its own light source from within. Its hands and feet were topped by vicious claws, long and acutely sharp. Dark gaudy veins ran the length of its exterior, crisscrossing its peculiar hue of pigmented skin, and its black, pupil-less eyes focused down into the cauldron.

Reaching out, the Keelut dropped a raw torn heart into the viscous liquid, followed by a liver of similarly wet and maimed condition. The organs floated for a moment in the fluid before slipping under the putrid surface.

For an extended time, the strange creature stared down, and its pulsing veins grew in intensity as the liquid boiled below. The beating thump of its body matched the throbbing light from the walls, as if the beast was in perfect harmony with the cavern itself, thrumming together as one entity.

Abruptly, the Keelut turned and moved back to the dark passage in the back wall. When it departed the expansive central area, the glow of the walls and shriek of far-off inhuman voices subsided, returning to their faint and eerie backdrop within the deep mountain chamber.

# Chapter Three

The embers were dying down in the campfire outside the church. Night intruded on the outdoor scene, forcing away the last of the wedding guests and making the location lonelier from their absence. The dull light of stars above drifting clouds provided scant illumination to the forlorn cow pastures in the nearby fields.

Rand, Sigri, Thorstein, and Galmand stood around the glowing remnants of the fire, enjoying the end of what was a pleasant celebration. Sigri stood in front of her taller husband, leaning back into his arms and snuggling close for warmth.

Behind her, Thorstein relaxed with Sigri in his arms, even as the whistle of a low-howling wind announced colder temperatures in their near future. His eyes were contemplative as he addressed the others, his deep-toned voice pronouncing his words with considered and respectful intent. "We'll first need to prepare our home here."

Rand stepped closer, ever vigilant for information regarding his beloved daughter's future. "You're staying for the entirety of the winter, correct? No reason to depart so soon—we have ample supplies."

There was a pause as each of the group considered Rand's words. It was apparent that Rand wasn't the only one wishing for the new couple to stay there, and whatever the party's inclinations were for respect, Thorstein would have to be wary of offending their desires for Thorstein and Sigri to remain in Greenland. Galmand nodded in silent agreement with Rand's wishes for them to remain local.

Thorstein smiled, keeping a tactful mood and ambiguous smile. "I have two of my best ships coming from Iceland. They are fully prepared—."

"Father, we're staying until the Spring," interrupted Sigri, not bothering to look back to Thorstein for approval. "No need to worry about me running away in the night."

Rand smiled and nodded, encouraged and contented for the time being. Thorstein offered him a reluctant grin, but he clearly wasn't enthusiastic about Sigri's promise.

Abruptly, the sound of a slow-squeaking cart came from the nearby forest. From down the wagon trail that made its way toward the church, the silhouette of an incoming wagon emerged from the low-lying mist. The wheel's creaky joints broke through the incessant whoosh of the distant wind, offering an early warning for the campfire party and making them focus into the night.

Tilting his head, Galmand squinted into the darkness, pointing toward two shapes walking near the small cart. "What visitor do we have at such a late hour? Who goes there?"

Emerging slowly from the darkness, Erik and Kristian walked into the faint light of the almost-depleted fire. As their features came into view, it was clear that neither was happy at visiting the recently completed wedding festivities. It wasn't a visit of well-wishers to the party.

As father and son came into clearer view, they stopped without greeting the priest and his guests. The four celebrants made eye contact with the pair, overtly confused at their late appearance there, a place they were not wanted or invited. On one hand, neither Thorstein nor Rand were happy with the interruption, while on the other, Sigri and Galmand were merely suspicious, seeming to wait for an explanation before judging Erik and Kristian's intentions.

Erik stayed quiet, frowning as he pointed to the back of the cart, where a simple blanket covered the lump of what could only be an unmoving body. The wind around them rose, as if a choir from nature had decided to mark their morbid visit with a chilling increase of the night's impending gale.

Kristian kept his eyes on the fire, studiously avoiding eye contact with any of the wedding party. It wasn't just the fact of the corpse that kept his standoffish eyes pasted on the fire, but also the overwhelming urge to engage with Sigri, to talk sense into her over this marriage madness. His chin quivered in the partial light of the fire as he fought for control over his raw emotions.

As their hosts registered what the dead body was, their worried faces moved between the wagon and its escorts, lost at what it could mean. Kristian and Erik remained silent, neither wanting to break the news of who lay below the tattered cloth to their side.

The pleasantries of the day's events wilted away, and Rand walked gingerly forward to move aside the blanket and see the identity of the deceased. When he pulled back the covering, all thoughts of marital bliss melted away, and his panicked eyes shot protectively back to his fearful daughter.

#

Backing through the sturdy wooden door, Erik grimaced as he sidled through the doorway from the night outside. He held the corpse under the armpits, with its vague outline still covered by the soggy blanket. Kristian struggled in after his father, holding the legs of the body as he shuffled into the constrained front room of Father Galmand's personal home. Both of their laboring faces showed disgust and worry at their unexpected delivery of waterlogged flesh to the holy priest's residence.

Grunting, Erik and Kristian heaved the deceased man onto a roughly hewn table in the middle of what passed for a living room. The lightly decorated walls of the house showed only a pleasant painting of Jesus and several crucifixes of various sizes to break up the chipped plaster on the uneven surface. Several lamps hung on posts throughout the space to provide sufficient light for the crowded area.

Galmand, Rand, and Thorstein stood a few feet back from the table, staring worriedly at the still-covered corpse, while Sigri peered from the doorway, a trembling hand covering her mortified face.

Erik slowly pulled the blanket back to reveal the body. Without saying a word, he motioned down to the white exposed flesh of the remains. The dead man's glassy eyes stared up at the ceiling, while his open mouth held what remained of a fish-chewed tongue. His abdomen was sliced neatly in a foot-long slit, and some coils of his intestines still protruded from the almost-empty confines of his trunk's cavity.

In answer to Erik's reveal of the cadaver, there was only troubled silence and distraught stares from their reluctant hosts. With nobody willing or able to talk, Erik sighed and leaned near Galmand, holding out a clerical collar. Galmand reached forward, gently taking it into his trembling fingers.

"Father Sturlesson…from the Western Settlement," said Galmand, and he turned the collar over in his hand, as if closer examination of the object could disclose some secret to the shocked room. His distressed gaze moved to the body of his fellow pastor, and he made the sign of the cross as he considered the pitiable corpse. "He wasn't due for another week. What brought him early, and what…happened to him?"

Erik backed away, assuming his place near his son against the wall. He focused respectfully on the corpse, then shook his head as he gestured to the closed door. "We don't know, Father. We found 'em in the Kangia, near where it meets the ocean. He was caught in our fishing net. After we drug 'em out, we went north for a bit, hugging the shoreline to figure out where he came from. We found a small rowboat about a mile up, where he must've come from the other settlement."

Perplexed, Rand cocked his head, glancing at the other onlookers with confusion. "I knew this man most of my life. He was a dedicated ambassador of the Lord. But…that's three hundred miles by boat, in icy seas—all by himself. Why would he do that, alone? And what happened to him? Killed by a bear, perhaps?"

Erik scowled, motioning to the dead priest. "His insides have been taken. A bear wouldn't take his guts without leaving a mark. There's no claw marks, and the organs were taken out with clean cuts. Like a gutted fish."

Stepping forward, Erik pointed at the uncovered feet of the body, where he indicated lacerations and bruises on his mangled toes and soles. "He must have been in a hurry to get away. He's either worn his boots off or had 'em torn away."

To the side, Kristian was silent, not keen to join the macabre conversation. He was, however, interested in Sigri, and he tried looking her way without being too obvious about it. Sigri didn't return the glance, but Thorstein noticed the younger man's attention. He moved to his new wife, blocking Kristian's view of her and pulling Sigri into a consoling hug.

Kristian looked away from the display of affection, and for a moment, it looked as if it was he who has had his heart removed.

Seeing Kristian's forlorn look, Erik rolled his eyes and clapped his son on the shoulder, bringing him back to the present as they faced the rest of the group.

Rand stepped forward and eased the blanket back over the remains, offering some dignity for the eviscerated priest in death. He shook his head and kept his voice low, almost pleading as he looked for an answer to the killing. "What could…how is this possible?"

After kissing Sigri on top of the head, Thorstein turned back to the late visitors to his wedding party. He met eyes with both, assuming a commanding voice as he talked, one that showed he was accustomed to being in charge. "This situation is terrible, but there must be an explanation. We mustn't allow this event to steal from our day of celebration. Accidents…happen every day in this harsh land."

For several moments, there was only silence in response. Each of the assembled group took turns staring at each other, while Sigri turned away entirely from the gathering. Tears streaked silently down her face as she tried to avoid witnesses to her crying.

Collecting himself, Erik shook his head and faced Thorstein. Trying to keep a respectful tone, he lowered his voice in a vain attempt to keep Sigri from hearing. "I don't think you understand. The "explanation" is we have a killer in the settlement, and he's a sick bastard. I don't need to tell you he needs to be found…or…"

As Erik trailed off, only frightened looks from the others answered his foreboding words.

# Chapter Four

The vast and open horizon was still lit by the day's sun, even as elongated light from the disappearing summer waned. Far into the distance, the broken and overcast sky was turning over, making the skyline appear restive and muddled under churning clouds.

Mountains in the distance were partially covered with a mesh of disheveled mist, looking like a clump of striated clouds had stopped just short of overflowing the untamed and icy peaks of their craggy outlines. Frosty howls of northerly winds swept across the sky, wailing in a chilly rush of raw arctic air to accompany the remote backdrop.

Below the airy atmosphere lay a great sheet of an enormous glacier. The contours of its cracking snow and broken ice stretched into the distance, providing a desolate scene across an unpopulated and wintry, snow-encrusted meadow.

To the west of the ice sheet, barely visible at the edge of the secluded scene, the rough seas of the Labrador Sea were covered in clumps of ice and turgid, lapping currents. Farther out, the ocean continued its unsettled and powerful movements, while directly on the edge of the snowy shoreline was a single canoe. The small craft was empty, but piles of supplies lay within its animal-skin confines.

Towards the interior of the ice floe, Seelah stood. Paused in the middle of this raw area, his eyes were open and alive as he focused ahead. Swathed in skins and padded primitive snowshoes, his native Inuit expression was well accustomed to the rigors of this harsh environment, only evincing a few wrinkles on his young features from the countless days spent under biting winds and glare-inducing snowfields.

Tipping his head towards the sky, Seelah let out a triumphant cry, one that echoed across the primitive environment, only briefly breaking the monopoly of shrieking gales around him. "Eeeeyaihhh."

As his confident bellow died away, Seelah refocused ahead. Only a few yards to his front, the clump of a mighty Polar bear lay on the ground, its great and now-bloodied form collapsed and motionless. Already dead, a spear protruded from its chest, and the direction and cant of its crumpled body showed that it was felled while attacking the Inuit hunter, trying to make a meal of the diminutive Seelah.

Seelah's victory over the fierce predator infused his demeanor with pride and excitement, and he beamed with the joy of the moment. He was alone in this frozen wasteland, but the challenges of a life spent pursuing such prey in this forbidding environment meant he needed to appreciate the moment, thanking the Gods for his chance to conquer such a dangerous beast. For several moments longer, he focused on the kill, basking in an accolade that he alone would cherish for a long time, though it would also surely make for a great story to share with his parents around a campfire at night.

Breathing deep, Seelah moved to the dead form of the bear, cautiously poking it with a long knife as he drew near. Seelah had heard of animals coming alive when they seemingly were already expired, and he knew that a simple swipe of a wounded animal like this could easily kill him, even if the bear itself was already mortally wounded. Caution was the hallmark of the Inuit hunter, who saved his strength and mental acuity for one great strike at his prey, while preferring to exercise vigilance at all other times.

Satisfied with the bear's condition, Seelah crouched over the beast to begin harvesting the kill. Withdrawing the spear with a clean pull, he plunged the weapon into a snowbank to the side, keeping its gory shaft within easy reach.

Turning back to the carcass, Seelah started by eviscerating the animal with a great slice of the abdomen, working around its plentiful musculature with precise cuts into the steaming abdomen. As he cut through gristle and innards, his face was focused and contented, the visage of a professional hunter fulfilling his duty to provide for his people.

As the shaman for his tribe, it was the role of Seelah to work in this way, to ply the fjords and ice floes of this area in pursuit of bears, seals, and fish. In this manner, the Gods would see his role as both honoring them and taking what is needed from their creation for his band of Inuit.

Seelah wore a bone necklace below his tightly wrapped sealskin jacket, and this jewelry was studded with the neck bones of various beasts he had long slain from the wild lands where they made their lives. Their spirits were now part of him, and he and his fellow natives cherished that closeness that could only be brought from consuming the meat of their treasured quarry.

His people were a hardy and persistent race that had carved out their existence from areas such as these since the origin of time, and Seelah felt great pride in ensuring their mastery of this difficult terrain would continue until the day his children's children would also partake of the Gods' goodwill. By finding their niche in this remote region, his people were perfectly suited to both enjoy nature's bounty and persist here until the world itself would come to an end.

From one hundred yards away, a slight movement came from a snowdrift, one that ran the length of the opposite side of the open ground where Seelah was crouched. The movement was just visible against the off-colored background of blue ice and pure white snow.

It was the Keelut, a form of predator that was decidedly unknown to the young Seelah. Its hideous bluish-white body shimmered a bit, then adjusted color to exactly match the environment directly behind it. Its horrifying face and body became perfectly camouflaged, indistinguishable from the harsh exterior world and utterly invisible to anyone looking for it.

As if sensing its presence, Seelah jerked upright from his labors at gutting his kill. He stood to survey his surroundings, panning his head to inspect the entirety of the open steppe around him. Seelah would never have made it to the ripe age of manhood in this ruthless world if he did not know that danger was near, and now, as he experienced this feeling of escalating tension, his insides pulsed with an awareness of peril he had never quite felt and couldn't entirely understand. He pursed his lips as he considered the solitary and frost-covered plains that surrounded him, wondering why his attention was drawn to the unoccupied wasteland.

Seelah reached over and plucked his spear from the snow, holding it up as he continued to scour the desolate snowbanks and open fields. He inclined his head, scanning for some sign of the trouble that his heart told him lurked out there. He felt something was indeed present, lurking on the periphery of his vision, and so he waited for some time, ready to meet the unseen hazard. As a man unafraid of what lurked in this dreary climate, he was more intrigued than scared by his increasing sense of alarm, and he turned in a circle, wary and ready for his silent watcher.

But nothing showed itself.

When no enemy made itself known, Seelah shrugged. Sighing, he returned to the dead bear, working again to cut free the parts most important to take to his canoe and back to his people. As he continued his grim work, his features softened and the unease faded from his distinctive features.

As the monotonous squishing of the animal harvest continued, the Keelut detached from its hiding spot, running at frightening speed toward Seelah. It was merely a blur on the open and snowy meadow, padding its strong legs silently across the ice as it closed the distance toward the unaware hunter.

Raising himself, Seelah once again felt that sense of disquiet, an odd pang of spooky warning that crept up his throat and prevented him from continuing his butchery of the bear. Turning about, his surprised eyes focused on the incoming predator, seeing only a vague blur as it closed the last few yards of distance. He was just able to raise his knife as his eyes grew wide, and the terrifying Keelut leapt upon him.

From high above, Seelah's shrieks carried across the wide and gloomy terrain, accompanied by grunts of his struggle and cries of his agony.

Then, silence. Only the incessant wail of neverending wind was again evident over the remote tundra.

#

The interior of the home was lavish and well-appointed. Deep-grained wooden furniture adorned the living room, providing a comfortable backdrop to large-curtained windows and the light that flowed through them.

Other curtains surrounded another set of windows that ran down one of the walls, and interspersed between each of them were gorgeous tapestries and fine paintings. The paintings depicted ancient kings and current genteel aristocrats, with Thorstein's serious and coy image looking particularly contented on one of the canvasses.

It was the residence of someone with both class and money, and whose owner was not afraid to show either. Amongst the sparse trappings common to homes on this humble and remote island, such a house was positively extravagant—the only one of its kind.

From that brace of side windows was a beautiful view of the ocean, and the construction of the house must have been particularly sighted to provide the breathtaking view of the eddied currents running toward the horizon.

Far to the side on the shoreline, where a deep copse of forest ran almost up to the edge of the water, a dock with several small boats was arranged. Various storage facilities were laid out around the path that led to those docks, and a collection of workers was just visible moving supplies back and forth between numerous commercial shacks.

Sigri sat in front of a desk looking over the roiling ocean, her mind lost in contemplation. She was bound up in fine clothing, wrapped for comfort in the warm and cozy home.

Her expression was not exactly unhappy, but neither was it the stuff of unrelenting joy.

Approaching from the side, Thorstein placed a sheaf of papers in front of her. His imploring eyes met hers as he motioned down to them. Sigri gazed back with features that could politely be described as stubborn.

Sigri glanced across the room, where a humble maid was dusting some plates stacked within a cabinet. With a polite gesture, she motioned for the maid to leave the area in order to give her and Thorstein some privacy. The confused teenage girl complied with a nod and shuffled out the open doorway.

"What you ask is too much," said Sigri, and she shook her head determinedly. "I can't leave my father…or my home. Not now, when he needs me most."

Thorstein grimaced, trying to remain patient. "I'm providing you with a beautiful home, as well as long-term prosperity for your father. He can come with us and have status, as well as material goods."

Sigri leaned back in her chair, looking at Thorstein with obvious disdain. She was clearly of another mind and not inclined to accept Thorstein's words at face value. "You told me we could live here. We have everything we could ever need HERE."

Thorstein sighed and paced away from Sigri, looking up at the ceiling and pondering how best to proceed with the discussion. Collecting his thoughts, he turned back to her and maintained a considerate tone. "I said we could make a home in Greenland. We could spend summers here, assuming it's possible…"

Sigri's face grew alarmed as Thorstein's words drifted off. "Possible? What do you mean?"

Thorstein thought for a moment, then sighed again. Motioning across the room, he walked over to an elaborate chess set perched on a shiny wooden table. The pieces on the board were exquisite and carved of ivory. Their detail and craft were remarkable, showing considerable effort and skill.

"Generations ago, this set was constructed from the tusks of the walrus," Thorstein said, and he shook his head slowly, admiring the work of the chessmen. "Tusks that were only available in Greenland."

Thorstein stepped away from the table and moved back to Sigri, stopping short of her and smiling affectionately. "Such a set would almost literally command the price of a King's ransom. Twenty men could not earn enough to buy it with a year of combined wages. Such was the value of just one of the commodities from these beasts that only inhabit this land."

Confused, Sigri glanced over to the chess table. She blinked several times as she took in Thorstein's words. "And what does this mean now?"

"But now, the world has changed, dear wife," said Thorstein, and he moved close to lean against her table, showing her his best salesman smile. "There's simply no demand for the tusks, at least to the extent that existed at one time. Instead, the markets of Europe are flooded with ivory from great beasts in Africa. It is said that quality and quantity are better, allowing for wider distribution of the fine material."

"People here are worth more than the pieces of a game," retorted Sigri, raising a disapproving eyebrow. "Even a king's game."

Thorstein acknowledged her words with a nod. "Yes, but the price of goods from this area affects Greenland's future. My shipments from this area have declined greatly over the last five years. I've been lucky to break even with the last few boats. It can't continue this way, or nobody will trade with this remote area."

Sigri stared up at Thorstein, unbowed by his negative assessment. "We've lived here for more than four hundred years. Our ancestors were feared across Europe. We will persevere in spite of these temporary…difficulties."

There was a crack in Thorstein's practiced exterior, and his empathy for his wife's position was briefly overcome with impatience. "Your ancestors are also from Iceland. It is Icelanders that settled this area, making it into what it...was. You can still make your history anew with our people from there."

Sigri wrinkled her nose and stood from the desk with a frown. She stared outside over the forever waves, pondering the vastness and beauty of her remote home at the edge of the settled world. Taking a deep breath, she pointedly avoided coming too close to her husband as she moved across the room to peer down at the chess set.

"Can I?" Sigri asks. "Will you also provide an estate for each of this village's craftsmen? For our farmers? Will they also have a place in our world in Iceland? Do we abandon people because they cannot provide the stuff of royalty's playthings?"

Thorstein's features deflated, and he took a moment to respond, sounding worried and fatalistic. "Sigri, I can't change the entire world, no man has that much property or money. I can only change our part in it."

Sigri nodded at his honesty but wasn't convinced. Reaching down, she toppled the king from the set with a single finger, letting the conversation die with the gesture. Pulling her shawl tight, she paced from the room without another word.

When she was gone, Thorstein shuffled the papers on the desk as he considered the conflict of warring loyalties that plagued his new wife's thoughts and aspirations. Anxious, he looked outside into the declining light, steeling his jaw in frustration.

#

Pale morning light surrounded a series of lonely outbuildings in the frosty countryside. Fog hung low on rocky fields that surrounded the crude structures, half obscuring a few goats that nibbled on the not-plentiful plants dotting its surface.

Ice dangled from limbs on stunted trees that encircled the farm, causing the forest around the homestead to take on a shriveled and pathetic appearance, as if the growth of plants and trunks had simply given up on their assigned task of growing larger.

To the interior of the large property was a functional home, one that obviously took great effort to maintain in the challenging and scrubby environment where it stood. An off-colored turf roof covered the house, and its exterior was whitewashed with simple paint to bring character to its doddering wooden walls. On the front of the house, a pair of shuttered windows were recessed to either side of a thick wooden door.

At a particularly rickety shack near the home, the ticking sound of struck metal echoed from inside, clanking with the beat of a hurried blacksmith. No chirping birds or sounds of wildlife filled the surrounding woods or meadows, making the call of chinking metal from within the place seem lonely.

That small structure was a basic stable. It was not spacious, and only two skinny horses and farm equipment populated the three stalls inside. Oil lamps cast jagged light across the dim interior, as the morning's burgeoning sunrays had not yet lit the corners of the darkish space. The low rush of a penetrating breeze evidenced the leaky nature of the exterior walls, with holes in the wooden planks showing that the time needed for maintenance was long past due.

Otherwise, there were functional workbenches and metal tools that decorated the interior, filling up the rest of the dusty area. Erik sat at the farthest bench to the back of the stable, leaning over an object and hitting it with a small ball-pean hammer. His mechanical strikes were methodical and precise as he focused down.

Finishing his work, Erik raised the dark metal edge of a crossbow bolt, admiring the sharp tip of the missile and twisting it around in the vague light to check that it was in good order for use. The glint of its jagged edge and barbed exterior showed it to be a deadly weapon for any potential adversary, and Erik imagined it burying into the neck of the homicidal maniac that had killed his friend, the priest.

Erik was not a violent man, but he recognized the need to protect those that are innocent. Living as a farmer in a remote village ensured some peace in life, but he was not so naive to believe that, even here, steps did not have to be taken for the proactive defense of oneself and his loved ones. He wouldn't be caught unaware, but he hated the idea that he had to feel this way in such a small and close-knit community.

From outside, the sounds of steps trudging closer to the building grabbed his attention, and Erik stared up at the flimsy entrance door. It eased open, and Kristian's curious gaze intruded on his weapon-making venture.

"Just like you said," said Kristian, stepping inside and shaking his head with worry. "Only half the milk we usually get."

Erik pursed his lips and frowned at the news. "Not good, son. It's just like everywhere else. We'll have to butcher 'em if this keeps up."

Kristian nodded, then cupped his hands to blow into them. Icy condensation from his breath made the attempt to keep warm seem futile, and he motioned outside to the other structures where the animals were kept. "Not enough hay. Not enough eggs. What are we going to do? Everything is icing up."

Erik laid down the crossbolt and rose, stretching his stooped back as he considered the question. He slowly shook his head as he considered the near future of the settlement. "This makes our seal hunt at Disko Bay more important than ever. The village will need all that meat to make it through the long winter."

Erik felt pained by this talk. As much as he hated it, their ability to control their lives' outcomes was growing more precarious each day. The temperatures and bad weather were making this year a difficult one. This long-lived Norse colony was difficult to survive in during the best of times but subsisting here had become increasingly desperate in recent times.

Still, Erik was not one to dwell on misery, so he walked near his son and clapped him on the shoulder. "We can only control what we do, not what happens around us. We've had plenty of tough times before, and we made out alright. Everything will be OK."

Kristian looked unconvinced, and after a moment of indecision, his gaze moved to the workbench. He walked near it and picked up one of several crossbow shafts Erik had been working on. "What are ya doin'?

Erik pointed down at the series of shafts and lowered his voice, his tone becoming more serious. "Making sure we're ready. You can never be too careful."

"Is it that serious," asked Kristian, showing an incredulous look. "You think it's someone in the town that killed the pastor?"

Erik didn't answer and instead moved toward a loft in the corner of the room. Only a bit of hay remained in it, and he heaved himself up a small latter, pulling down a tattered leather bag from underneath what remained.

Kristian looked surprised, apparently not knowing the long leather bag was there. He watched Erik set it on the floor with an intrigued stare.

"These have been in the family since before my grandfather's time," Erik said, and from the bag, he withdrew two scabbarded weapons: a long sword and a shorter, thin knife. "From long ago, when being armed was a matter of survival."

Erik pulled out each blade with a SCHIIK, holding the longer weapon in his strong arm and flipping the other around to give to his son, hilt-first. Kristian took the offered knife with a reserved frown and examined its clean and sharp edge in the subdued light. The fact that the weapon had been maintained and cleaned by his father without Kristian's knowledge was not lost on him—Erik was full of surprises.

"My father told me these were used even before Christ was brought to the remotest regions of Norway," said Erik, and he examined the sharp edge of his own blade before continuing. "In fact, it was said that these blades were brought there from the first holy knights, ones that evangelized our backward ancestors. They came when all manner of evil and sin infected the people."

Pointing to the pommel of the longsword, Erik indicated a Christian cross, then pointed at the same religious insignia on the handle of the knife he handed his son. "These were meant to protect the bearers in battle, so that the health and souls of fighters could be protected."

Kristian stayed quiet, taking in his father's words while staying focused on his newly acquired blade.

Leaning down, Erik re-sheathed the sword, becoming contemplative. "And now that time is here again. The need to watch out for each other and our neighbors can be served with these ancient things. From now on, we go nowhere alone, and you have to keep your eyes and ears open. Our lives—and others—depend on it."

Standing to his full straightened height, Erik gazed at the long knife Kristian held, then peered deep into his son's eyes. The concerned gaze of a protective father watched Kristian in the now-silent room, and the gravity of the moment wasn't lost on Kristian.

Nodding, Kristian could only gulp in response.

# Chapter Five

Under the overcast afternoon light, there stood a not-busy market area in the middle of the Eastern Settlement. Numerous stalls full of basic foodstuffs and tawdry equipment were spaced throughout the open-air space, with only a few village residents rummaging through mostly dilapidated household articles laid out to entice shoppers.

Products ranging from crude children's dolls to half-broken tools made up most of the items, while overpriced meats and scrumptious pastries from enterprising cooks were unfortunately too expensive for majority of the people in close proximity to their delectable smells.

Around the primary selling area were many empty booths, as if the lack of commercial interest had halted any expanded trade from the merchant class in the village.

Because the selection of usable goods wasn't expansive, the vendors standing next to the items looked neither cheerful nor optimistic about their economic prospects. Frowns covered their unshaven faces and their desperate sellers' eyes focused on the few prospective buyers that perused the merchandise, imploring them for even a small purchase.

Little conversation or pleasant interaction flowed through the depressing communal area, making the poor environment seem even more constricting than the blighted economic conditions should have dictated.

Erik and Kristian paced next to the line of informal shops, their gazes moving over the varied commodities offered for sale. After a long search, they finally found a stall that caught their interest, where aged weapons and cheap armor were laid out on creaky tables.

From behind the items, a dour middle-aged man with weathered spectacles and poor dental hygiene eyed the duo, licking his lips in groveling anticipation of them browsing his wares.

Ignoring the seller, Erik pointed down at some materials and motioned to his son. Kristian nodded and sorted through some wooden shields and rusted daggers, hoping to find something of interest for their defensive preparations. Nothing seemed very usable, though, and Kristian scowled in frustration at the prospects, shaking his head at his father in disappointment.

Erik's attentive eye caught on something piled amongst several old and disused bags to the side. Walking over towards the cache of mismatched material, Erik focused on the end of the last table of the vendor. As Kristian joined him, Erik began rummaging through some leather knickknacks.

Intrigued, Erik held up a pair of stiff leather-armored gloves, and several more matching ones lay beyond it in a pile. Slipping his hands into each glove, he flexed his fingers inside, wiggling them to ensure a proper fit. They were long enough to almost reach his elbows and covered his forearms well.

Pointing to Kristian's knife, Erik asked him to hand it over with a nod of his head. When Kristian gave it to him, Erik ran the edge of the sharp blade over the hard leather of both gloves. The material's surface was unaffected by the slicing action, showing its impressive protective qualities. Erik nodded approvingly at the firm gauntlets, then removed and dropped them on the table.

Seeing his opportunity, the merchant scurried over, happy for the chance at some business from the father and son. "That's sure to keep ye safe. They used to use 'em in the battles in the Holy Land. Saved many a fighter from losin' a limb. It's even got the Crusade mark on it."

The vendor pointed to a cross-like mark stenciled on the hard surface of the leather. After running his finger over the mark, Erik pondered for a moment, returning the knife to his son and fixing his gaze on the owner of the makeshift shop.

"I'll take two sets of 'em, as long as you give me a discount on the second pair," Erik said, and he motioned to his son with a grin. Kristian returned the grin with an appreciative smile, happy to be getting his own set of hand protection in the deal.

The seller feigned a look that said *You're taking food from my kids' mouths,* but he also nodded with relief at finally having an offer for a sale. He held up four fingers to indicate the hoped-for price, clearly anxious that the amount didn't chase away Erik's potential business.

Not one to pass up a good deal, Erik kept his smile and removed a pouch from his waistband. He shuffled four copper coins into the waiting hand of the vendor, patting the man on the shoulder in an affectionate sign of village solidarity.

From behind, a hand suddenly grabbed Erik's shoulder, jostling him in surprise and interrupting the transaction. Erik raised his eyebrows in alarm as he spun around to meet the annoying interloper.

A weathered Inuit man stood before him, his mischievous eyes matching his amused lips in a conspiratorial smile. Iqiak continued to grin up at the tall Erik, then moved his gaze to the even-taller Kristian. Dressed smartly in puffy animal skins, the squat-but-powerful Native had the kind bearing of a man who could charm a carcass from the clutches of a pack of wild dogs.

Erik's features filled with friendly recognition, and he embraced Iqiak in an enthusiastic man-hug. To the side, Kristian grinned broadly at the happy spectacle, glad for the chance to see and chat with his father's oldest friend.

#

The bar was a humble place, with plain wooden benches surrounding several worn tables throughout a cramped main hall. On the timbered walls were several simple paintings, and the topic for the artwork seemed to be white wolves, the roaming predator that made a home on much of the arctic tundra.

On each of the flat-painted boards were crude depictions of the arctic wolf with a white fluffy coat and a mean, snarling maw. It gave the interior of the cramped area a bit of a creepy feeling, like it was set up to worship the vicious and bloodthirsty predator.

The establishment was not busy at this time of day, and only Erik, Kristian, and Iqiak sat at a table in the middle of the room. Pale light shone through a set of windows that looked out over the largely uninhabited market outside, while the three men gazed at one another across the table with the genial gazes of familiar acquaintances.

Behind them, a barkeep stood alone behind a narrow benchtop, chopping slices of bread with a disinterested frown. The creaking legs of his stool, which buttressed the man's considerably weighty frame, was the only sound to fill the dimly lit area.

Looking at his friends, Iqiak took a swig from his tattered mug, then grimaced at the bitter brew and its less-than-savory aftertaste. "I never understood how you drink this…liquid. It has bad taste."

Erik grunted a series of low, amused chuckles at the disgusted look on Iqiak's timeworn features. "The more you drink, the better it is. By the end of our night, you won't remember what any of it tasted like. I promise yeh, later today you'll think it the best concoction you've ever gagged down."

Kristian nodded in agreement to the side, matching his father's grin with a pleasant and lively expression. "Besides, you drink seal's blood yourself. Not exactly refreshing, right?"

Iqiak thought for a moment, focusing up at the ceiling and carefully considering those words. He turned to peer at Kristian, holding out a clenched fist that mimicked an erect penis. "Seal blood keeps a man healthy—and strong."

Erik and Iqiak erupted in a gout of laughter, and Erik clapped Iqiak on the shoulder, nodding at the strength of his argument for virility. It took some time for the laughs to die down, and all the while, Kristian's face was deep red with embarrassment.

When their chuckles lessened, Erik's face lost its amusement. He stared meaningfully at Iqiak, intense and suddenly worried. He could feel something under the surface of Iqiak's presence here and wanted to get to the truth of the visit. "What brings you to town? We weren't expecting you until next month—after the hunt to Disko Bay."

Iqiak looked down at his hands, letting the enjoyable mood die away as quickly as it had come. "We have hunter that go missing. We hope he came to you. Maybe he trade something, maybe visit a woman here in village. His name is Seelah, and his family worried."

Erik and Kristian went quiet as they traded concerned glances. Kristian pursed his lips in worry and looked toward one of the windows, while his father focused at Iqiak.

"We haven't seen 'em," said Erik. "But we'll keep an eye out for him. How long since one of your people contacted this…Seelah?"

Disappointed, Iqiak frowned and took a sip of his cheap drink. Swirling the liquid around in his mouth, he swallowed with a frown. "A few days. This is not good. Maybe a white bear caught him."

Erik offered his friend a sympathetic frown. Going missing on a hunt was not unheard of, even for the skilled Inuit, but it pained him to see Iqiak mourning over the man's disappearance. The nature of the Inuit life meant it was even more hazardous than the farm life of the Norse Greenlanders, but that didn't make a missing hunter any less tragic.

Leaning forward, Erik lowered his voice, fixing Iqiak with a serious and troubled face. "Speaking of missing, we found a priest from the Western Settlement in the river. We were lucky to find the body. Worse thing is, he'd been killed by someone, his insides cut out…"

Iqiak reached out abruptly, his powerful hand grabbing Erik's forearm in a fierce grip. Erik flinched at the pressure, and

Kristian peered at Iqiak with an anxious stare, puzzling over what was wrong.

"You have dead shaman?" asked Iqiak, and his face was a mask of trepidation, with his lined wrinkles framing an uneasy and dark expression. "His organs are missing? Taken from body?"

Erik and Kristian both nodded, not sure of what to say, so they instead opted for quietness. As time ticked on, the silence even got the barkeep's attention, who frowned over at the small party.

"What is it?" Erik asked, finally breaking the disturbed and tense atmosphere. "Do you know who could've…?"

Iqiak released his friend's arm as Erik's words dropped away. In shock and at a loss for words, Iqiak appeared incapable of continuing.

Iqiak's crestfallen gaze moved out the window as his distraught features pondered the suddenly mysterious events surrounding his visit to the settlement.

#

The wagon trail twisted through a misty forest, its meandering track of soil and frosty rock well lit under the early afternoon sky. The Birch trees to either side of the worn pathway leaned at odd angles, their branches weighed down by frost that had yet to be burned away from the rays of sun streaming through the canopy of twigs and leaves overhead.

The floor of the icy earth cracked under the gentle wheels of Erik's simple donkey and cart. The animal pulled the vessel with unenthusiastic lunges as it huffed its way forward, clearly not happy with the laborious effort of hauling goods. The lumbering cart was full of chopped wood and coils of rope, the latter having been twisted together from the hides of numerous walruses, sea animals that were a staple of Greenland's exports.

In front of the cart walked Erik, who paced ahead with a pleasant-enough look, one that belied the troubles facing him and his son. Erik had always had a sense that the life he led was part of a play, a play that included moments of tragedy and abject sorrow—but was nevertheless entertaining if you approached it the right way. Further, he thought of his role in life as a harbinger of what could be: simple people could really make a difference in the world, always making for a better tomorrow than the day before.

Work alone was not what made a man decent, but it was a significant part of what made you better. Keeping your nose down and focusing on family and good thoughts are what offered him promise, both here and in the afterlife. Keep it simple, Erik thought, because complicating things always seemed to be what got people in trouble with themselves—and with the world around them.

Erik had always noticed that having nothing to do, either from being rich or simply lazy, never did anyone any good. Whether chopping wood or doing any of the thousand things that always needed his efforts on the farm, he knew he was at his happiest when staying busy. Fruitful labor made a man focus inside, especially when it was done right and with the proper attitude.

In Erik's own way, he almost pitied those who had it otherwise. His favorite homily from Father Galmand was when the priest quoted the ancient words of Saint Gerome, who wisely proclaimed, "It is idle to play the lyre for an ass." Wasting one's time for pursuits that were neither good nor enlightening were not expressions of time well spent, and it rarely made a person better or more contented.

Erik knew that his son felt otherwise—Kristian always had his head in the clouds, thinking of unattainable pursuits and childish notions of love—but he felt it was his job to help Kristian learn otherwise. That had to be why God put him on earth, to cultivate his son's place in the world. To always help him.

Smiling, Erik stopped and looked behind the cart, where a dark-cloaked Kristian walked with a sour grimace, the look that always said, *woe is me.*

His son, wondering why Erik stopped, pulled up short and frowned at his father. The woods around them were quiet, and no birds or animals were evident in the considerable foliage.

Kristian must have thought Erik was pondering their encounter with Iqiak. He spoke in a halting voice while staring at his father across the cart and donkey. "What do you think it means? With Iqiak?"

Now, Erik frowned, and his thoughts were also pulled back to his old friend. "Iqiak? I think he's afraid, and I don't know what he could be afraid of. I've known him for twenty years and never seem 'em scared of anything. It's even worse that he doesn't want to talk about it. Kind of makes me worried, to be honest."

Kristian nodded, agreeing with a shrug to those sentiments. After a moment of silence, he changed the subject, but his voice devolved into a whine. "When we get there, can you take the goods inside? I really don't want to see…"

Erik held his hand up, gently silencing Kristian. He used the silence to focus his attention entirely on his son, making sure he had Kristian's full attention. "Son, you're gonna have to get over this. It's not the right way to act, pining for another man's wife. I've taught ya better."

Kristian turned his eyes to the forest, shame wearing down on his depressed features.

Erik moved the conversation in another direction, lightening his expression and adopting an instructive tone. He hoped he sounded fatherly, but he could never really tell—emotions really weren't his specialty. "Let me tell you a story. Unlike most of 'em, you haven't heard this one before."

Erik slapped the donkey and started walking again. As the animal trundled on, Kristian moved up to his father's side, matching his pace. The cart's wheels squeaked as Erik took a deep, reflective breath. "Back in Norway, before I met your mother, our farm was poor. Life was hard, and my parents had no money or social standing."

Kristian glanced over at Erik, surprised at the direction of the conversation.

"My father was drunk most of the time, so I had to do all the work," Erik said, and he tightened his lips as an inner surge of sorrow filled his guts. "It was a tough way to live."

Walking in silence for several moments, Erik collected himself, but his voice cracked as he continued, making his words uneven and quiet. "When my mother died, I had to take care of everything. My father laid in bed all day because he didn't care about anything. He wasted away in grief because he knew he'd been a bad husband. He died a sad death by himself, while I was working in the fields."

Erik walked for a time, taking a while to stamp out the lingering sadness from his thoughts. "Anyway, after that, one day while delivering food to town, I met a girl…Gunilla. She was something to behold—a real looker. I was smitten."

Kristian's eyes bulged in response to this revelation, clearly shocked that Erik could have ever been young—or interested in another woman. Erik merely shrugged at the admission, knowing there could be no harm in his son seeing him as human. It might even help to get his point through Kristian's thick skull.

"So, I decided she was to be my wife," continued Erik, and the foggy memories from the distant time parted a little, allowing those childish desires to become real in his mind. For a moment,

Erik could almost feel like he was there, blushing at that blond woman in a long-forgotten market in a country he hadn't seen for thirty years. "Problem was, her family would rather have killed me than let such a thing happen."

"Wh...what happened," Kristian asked, obviously intrigued.

"Well, they ran me out of town—I barely escaped with my life. Had to move to Nidaros, because Gunilla's Chieftain husband-to-be wanted my head, literally—simply for my young-man's desires."

From ahead, to the side of the barren road, the Keelut watched as father and son approached. Camouflaged amongst bushes and stands of trees, it was entirely invisible to the pair, its imperceptible outline lost in a cluster of undergrowth.

Erik and Kristian strode on, but the donkey caught the scent of this unseen danger. Stopping, the animal flinched, its nostrils flaring at the smell of their watcher. It neighed a fearful snort as it shook its head uneasily from side to side.

Stopping, Erik became confused. He strode to the animal and stroked its neck, then panned around to look for what bothered it. Kristian also felt it, something that portended risk at the periphery of his inner understanding of how the world worked. Some primeval warning signal was firing in his brain, using his base sense of fear to inform Kristian's conscious mind.

Moving to his son's side, Erik put his hand on the hilt of his sword, spinning around to scan the thick forest for danger. Kristian joined him in scouring the area, pulling the knife from his waist scabbard and ensuring he faced the opposite way from his father. The effect was there was no way they could be sneaked up on.

Erik was staring at their silent stalker, and he tilted his head in confusion as his eyes investigated the confines of the underbrush and the outlines of trees. The creature was right in front of him.

The Keelut did not move as it remained hidden from normal vision. It focused on Erik as it awaited his next action, almost as if daring him to see its shrouded form.

The disquiet and sense of dread in Erik were matched by the fear in Kristian's face, a fear that grew as the silence continued. While the unseen creature watched them, they both knew on some inner level it was there, waiting and watching. Unfortunately, their overt faculties saw or heard nothing.

The Keelut continued its overwatch of the duo, but its vision focused particularly on the weapons each man carried. For a long while, it silently stared, taking in the moment like an always-aware predator, ready to pounce in a moment—or to bide its time for a better opportunity to make its kill.

Unable to see a threat, Erik eventually gave up looking, and he slapped their porter-animal several times to get it moving. With a snort, it eventually moved on, but its steps were imperfect and awkward as it struggled ahead to get cart's heavy load moving.

As they resumed their pace away from the Keelut, the creature stayed silent and still, its despicable and sentient eyes peered at its potential prey. It did not move to follow, but its dark pupil-less orbs focused after them in acute interest, the interest of a hunter. A patient and deadly one.

In time, a sense of calm returned to Erik's face, and he felt foolish for this foray into paranoia. Sighing, he resumed the conversation, using one last glance around them to verify nobody or nothing was following. "It was better in the end, so everything worked out. I met the world's best woman six months later, your loving mother. She was a seamstress at a place I regularly delivered milk to. We left Norway together a year later, hoping to find a slice of success in this faraway land. You were born a while after we came here. Fate has a way of fixing things in life that were never meant to be."

Trying to relax, Erik raised his voice a bit, just enough to show Kristian what came next was of the highest importance. "The point is, son, don't expect the world to suffer your wants and desires, just because you don't mean anything bad by it. There was once a man, Kolgrim was his name, from far over at the West Fjord, near the last line of valleys next to the tundra. Maybe fifteen years ago, he seduced a woman who was married to a Chief out that way, before that whole area was abandoned. You know what happened to 'em when they were found out?"

Kristian shook his head, a look of worry filling his face. Stopping, he peered over at his father, and Erik also halted to stare sideways.

Erik sought out Kristian's anxious eyes, trying to reach through the raw feelings that colored Kristian's perception of the world. If Erik was to be successful in coaching his son, he had to reach him with pure logic—and perhaps a bit of fear.

"He was burned alive at the stake by the husband's clan, and there wasn't a thing his family could do about it," Erik said. "The Chieftain's clan accused him of sorcery, and the church stood aside while it happened, powerless to stop a clan with money and control of the sheriff. The "sorcery" was really only the lust of forbidden lovers, but that didn't save Kolgrim. He was burned to ashes."

At this news, Erik clapped Kristian on the shoulder and moved on. Better to leave him with that disturbing image, Erik thought—anything to get through to him.

Kristian waited a moment before following, taking in the gravity of his words as his father paced away. Focusing on the rocky ground before him, Kristian started after Erik. As the young man's troubled eyes mulled through their recent discussion, he was no longer interested in talking.

As father and son plodded ahead, the Keelut watched them disappear down the remote trail.

#

Foamy ocean surf crashed against a jagged shoreline, surging over its dark timeworn rocks and retreating to open water in sudsy rivulets. Successive waves of the dark sea's frothy saltwater battered the coast in never-ending rhythms, resounding across the remote strip of coastline in a cadenced roar.

In the distance, a low fog hung over the vast ocean, while on the shore, an assortment of warehouses was perched on a seaside bluff. These storage facilities were extensive and were meant to quarter goods being readied for export from the Eastern Settlement to the markets of Europe, which typically included items such as tusks, furs, and cattle hides. Tellingly, only two of the ten stone buildings were currently being used, while the rest were chained up and unattended.

A functional wagon trail led down to a dock that floated in a natural harbor, a wide and calm area that offered protection from the swells of seething currents that lay beyond it. The recurring sound of breaking waves along the harbor's exterior was interspersed with the occasional chatter of seagulls, while a few workers stacked goods in small boats that served as delivery barges for tiny villages at other places along the nearby ocean coastline.

The largest of the operating warehouses was a substantial structure. Surrounded by a clearcut area marked with tree stumps and clumps of sparse grass, it had wagons and stacks of supplies lined up and prepared for loading.

This main stone structure had a set of large open doors leading to an interior full of barrels and crates of goods. One side of the interior storage was occupied by imports from abroad, while the other was piled high with exports for far-distant lands. The import side was markedly less crowded, and it had empty gaps among its stacked materials set for distribution throughout the Greenland colony.

At the entrance to the warehouse, Thorstein sat under a wooden eave behind a formidable handmade desk. Thick and seemingly made to withstand even the worst natural disaster, the enormous desk made him seem scrawny and insubstantial behind it. Focusing down, Thorstein leafed through several papers, stopping to read lists of assigned items for dispersal or packing.

Erik and Kristian approached the entrance and stopped their cart in the area adjacent to the open door. Over the next several minutes, they unloaded their supplies and carefully stacked them inside. Both father and son hoisted the wood and rope, ensuring it was neatly organized, while Thorstein made an obvious effort to ignore them. No pleasantries or words of greeting were exchanged as they worked, and the only sound came from Thorstein's writing quill as he scrawled addendums in the ledgers laid out before him.

When done, Erik approached the desk, trying to be humble as he waited to be addressed. Thorstein took his time acknowledging him, pausing to sort through sheaves of accounting documents.

"Is that everything, then?" asked Thorstein, and he still didn't raise his gaze to Erik.

"Yeah, that should do it," replied Erik, and he looked behind himself, where Kristian was skulking outside by their cart. "It's everything you asked for."

Thorstein cast a disdainful look at Kristian before looking inside at the delivered goods. "I can see that…but I can also see a young man who lets his eyes wander, who focuses his attention on things that are not his…and never will be. It's not a pleasant or respectable way to represent your family."

Stung by the insult to his family honor, Erik looked back to Kristian and shook his head in frustration. The accusation was made worse by its truth, and he didn't want to degrade the situation further by lying about it. "Yes, well, I want to apologize for that. He and your wife grew up together…so I—."

Thorstein raised a silencing finger, dropping all pretenses of kindness towards Erik. He gestured to Kristian but locked his gaze solely on Erik. "That is not something that really interests me, nor should it. I only have interest in proper respect, and that's not forthcoming from you."

Erik knew this could happen, where Kristian's youthful romance could lead to serious repercussions, even if there wasn't currently a real relationship to back it up. He had seen men die for less in his time, and he tried to appear servile in order to tamp down the burgeoning problem. "Thorstein, I am aware how it could seem, but there is nothing—."

Thorstein cut him off by pounding the table and raising his voice. "How exactly would you deal with the problem, Erik? If a man had designs on your wife? What should be the remedy for such insolence?"

Erik pondered that and moved his eyes to the table. He shifted his weight from one foot to another as he collected his thoughts, brooding over the best way forward. "I would be reasonable. We were all young once, and there is no bad intention toward you or your wife."

Thorstein leaned back against his chair, chuckling bitterly. "I am a reasonable man, which is a good thing for you and your family. If this is something I need to address again, the results will be neither reasonable nor mild. I think you know that. In fact, I'm counting on you knowing that, so there will be no more unpleasantness for me to deal with."

Thorstein stood and fixed Erik with a threatening stare. Taking a pouch of coins from his deep-pocketed and expensive shirt, he cast it across the desk, where it clinked and settled on the edge of the pricey wood. "In the meantime, this will be the last business we conduct. I will find my suppliers elsewhere. Honorable men are an essential part of any transaction, and that isn't…you."

Sitting back down, Thorstein returned to his ledger, ending the discussion.

Erik had known this business with Thorstein could be tricky, but he paled with the thought of losing work from the settlement's richest man because of it. Erik was the best all-around worker in the village, and he had hoped for Thorstein to realize that and be rational about this issue with his son.

Instead, it had become progressively worse, and now Erik was at a crossroads of sorts, not knowing what to do or say. The reality was that when pride and love were involved, rationality was thrown out the window—even among cultured and wealthy men.

Erik cleared his throat to speak, hoping to make a plea for reconsideration, but Thorstein waved him away with a dismissive scowl.

In shock, Erik grabbed the coin pouch and turned back to their cart. Kristian waited there, his nervous eyes focusing on his father as he wondered what exactly had just transpired. Exasperated, Erik grabbed the reigns of the donkey and paced away from the warehouse, avoiding his son's distressed gaze as he hurried away.

# Chapter Six

No signs of life were evident on the remote farm. Winds blew across matted clumps of grass in derelict pastures surrounding a series of wooden buildings topped with turf roofs and shoddy wooden walls. Frost covered the entirety of the land and structures, showing a white sheen across the lonely landscape, as if it had all been dipped in water and then frozen in time.

Above, the sky swirled with gray and dense cloud cover, blotting out all evidence of blue sky or any bright rays of the sun. The rapid advance of the intimidating clouds immersed the local climate in a roiling sense of impending demise, where calamity seemed to lie just underneath the surface of this isolated stretch of deteriorating farmland.

The wailing cry of a freezing wind provided the area an isolating auditory atmosphere, even more so than should have been evident from the icy fields and empty sheep and cattle corrals. As if to accentuate the sense of lonely despair, a barn door banged intermittently against its broken frame, swaying with the on-and-off surge of forceful drafts that swept across the surrounding meadows.

Two men leaned forward on horses as they picked their way toward the main building on the farm. Ketil was in the lead, eying the living quarters warily, while Sigmar trailed close behind, plodding along and scanning the area to either side for signs of life. Ketil was a bear of a man, armed with a great sword across his back, and while Sigmar was smaller of stature, he was also well-armed and armored, ready for whatever awaited them.

Together, the gruff men, covered in raggedy beards and sour demeanors, pulled up short of the house. Looking worried, their eyes sought answers, scouring the surroundings for anything amiss. Sitting still, they finally focused on the door, waiting as if they soon expected someone or something to run out in greeting.

Nobody emerged to hail them, and the old warriors scowled in disappointment. After some time, their irritable dispositions grew sad from the lack of welcome by any inhabitants of the home.

Sighing, Ketil dismounted with a grunt and looked up at his frowning companion. "No one's seen 'em for two weeks. Not like 'em to hole up here…without any contact."

Sigmar grunted and also came down from his horse. He nodded a pained agreement, then gestured to the nearest barn with his head. "Check out the barn. Be careful, something isn't right. I can feel it in my bones, just like when I can sense bad weather comin' on."

Ketil frowned even further, drawing his lips tight as he considered the worrying circumstances of their visit. He was a man who had not often known fear, something which made him the perfect partner for Sigmar, his grizzled friend and functioning co-sheriff for the entire extended village. Together, they had been known as the law and enforcers of peace in the Eastern Settlement for the better part of two decades, but because they were well-liked and respected, violence was a trade they didn't often need to practice. Ketil had an uneasy feeling this long period of peace was going to end soon, and he didn't like how that made him feel.

After tying his horse to a post, Ketil reached into a side pack on the animal and withdrew an old and battered lamp. Taking a minute, he concentrated and lit it, then held it up to look across the front yard at the barn. Unsheathing the large sword from his back, he sighed and paced toward the lonely and dark structure, his blade held up and ready.

Breathing deep, Sigmar watched Ketil go with an apprehensive grimace, wondering what trouble had befallen this outlying farm. He had known the owner Halfdan for many years, since they were both young boys beating each other with wooden practice swords. Their sons played together when the weather allowed, and his wife was friendly with Halfdan's own lady.

It was not often that a man had a chance to call someone a true friend in this frontier life, but in the case of Halfdan, there was a real and close bond, the type reserved for only a few others in the village.

Sigmar pulled a torch from his leather pack and lit it with a tinder box. Holding the fire in front of the door, his eyes moved to a small window at the side, and he took in the fact that no light escaped from the interior of the house. Detaching a small ax from his waist, he hefted and tested the weight with practiced slices of the air.

Extending the metal-pointed end of his sharp weapon, Sigmar banged the solid door with several hard taps. "Halfdan…you there? We haven't seen ye for a couple weeks. Got worried, so we thought we'd check on you and your family."

No sound came from inside to answer his query—no grunting or shuffling of feet toward the door to acknowledge his presence. It appeared as if the homestead had been deserted. Nobody ever deserted their homes in Greenland, and when you went somewhere, you told neighbors…just in case they had to find you later. There was never a surplus of acquaintances at the end of the settled world, so a farm being deserted was a very bad sign.

Licking his lips in worried anticipation, Sigmar's jaw hardened, and he leaned forward to turn the cold door handle. The door swung inward, creaking with the disconcerting squeal of rusted hinges. The interior was not huge, and sufficient light from the overcast day and torchlight mostly illuminated the area inside.

Stooping low, Sigmar moved the crackling flame ahead, lighting up the darker corners of the room as he stepped inside. It was a standard-sized and basic front room for the Norse, a place with simple furnishings and benches covered with animal skins. A sewing area with looms for mending clothes and crafting new shirts and dresses was in one corner, but nobody was there to do such work at the present. A brightly painted but crude shield with a family insignia hung from one wall, while some farm tools were suspended from two others.

To the side was a kitchen area with a place to hang pots over a fire pit when preparing meals. Farther to the back, near a rough cabinet with basic utensils and pots, another smaller table stood. This was the principal place to serve food for families when guests were not present, a private area where only the family usually took their meals.

Nobody was here. It was empty and quiet.

Stepping into the kitchen area, Sigmar held his torch over the table. On the top of it were two bowls of old soup, full of a half-eaten meat porridge and congealed broth. They looked to have been there for some time, abandoned during the middle of a meal.

Next to one of the bowls was a large smear of dark, solidified substance. Black in color, it was unidentifiable and viscous, not matching anything around it. Sigmar wrinkled his nose as he stared down, somehow disturbed by the unknown material.

Sigmar held his ax down, scraping up some of the firmed-up liquid with the top point of his weapon. Holding the ax up, he sniffed the substance. The foul smell of whatever it was assaulted his nose with a pungent death-like odor, and he held it away from his face with a disgusted grimace. Producing a grimy rag from his belt pouch, he cleaned off his ax and moved his gaze to the floor of the kitchen area.

Crouching down, Sigmar examined shattered cups and a broken cross, all of which had been thrown about the hardened dirt floor, as if a desperate fight had occurred here. Worse, blood spatters accompanied the struggle, and from the amount of dried blood, it was apparent it hadn't ended well for whomever was injured.

Gulping, Sigmar righted himself and focused on a hallway leading to the back of the home. Moving slowly, he edged to the dark hall, holding up the torch as he crept ahead.

His light illuminated splatters of more blood on the walls' surface. Chaotic and gory, it appeared like buckets of the stuff had been splashed about, like it was thrown around to paint the area completely.

His arm shaking, Sigmar approached the back room, where a simple door had been broken from the entryway, showing the sleeping area beyond. As he pushed aside the remnants of the door, his gaze fell upon the remains of the room. Here, there were three straw-stuffed mattresses cast about, their outside covered in yet more blood. On the floor, personal items and clothing were strewn amidst more gore, and a crude dresser lay overturned in the disordered area.

A child's doll lay abandoned in the middle of the floor, also caked with black-crusted blood.

But there were no bodies, just what remained of some endless carnage. Sigmar moved gently through the room, looking hopelessly for his friend and family in the discarded and shattered refuse of their lives.

From behind, the silence of the traumatic moment was interrupted by Ketil clearing his throat. Sigmar flinched at the sound and turned to see Ketil standing in the broken doorway. Ketil's sword was still drawn, and his haunted eyes looked about the room Sigmar stood in, equally bothered by what he saw.

Strangely, Ketil wasn't wearing his cloak. As his gaze met Sigmar's, he shook his enormous head and motioned behind—toward the front of the home. "You need to see this, Sigmar. Someone really bad has been to this place."

#

Sigmar stared down, his rough and weathered features perplexed and anxious. He focused with the expression of one who couldn't understand what he saw, like he needed time to mull over some wretched and unknowable experience. Taking several deep and haggard breaths, he turned away, and rubbing his fingers through his tangled beard, he paced the floor and fought the urge to scream in anger.

On a bench in the front room sat Magnus, Halfdan's son. The eight-year-old sat calm and unemotional, smothered in Ketil's warm bearskin cloak. Though gaunt and dirty, the child was apparently healthy, but he also looked straight through Sigmar, his vision and perception stuck somewhere else—like his mind had decided to vacate the physical world.

Looking to the side, Sigmar met Ketil's eyes, searching for some reasoning that could explain this broken child, an innocent and now catatonic victim of unknown circumstances. Staring back, Ketil looked ashen and confused as he also tried to get at the meaning of what they were witnessing.

Some time passed as they traded stares.

Breathing in throaty rasps, Ketil was as frustrated as Sigmar, and he spoke with a halting and disquieted tone. "Found 'em in the hay, I could barely see 'em there…with it all piled around him. He had some crusts of half-eaten bread and dirty blankets. He was lyin' in his own filth."

Leaning down, Sigmar snapped his fingers in front of the boy's eyes. Magnus didn't respond—his consciousness remained elsewhere. Standing straight, Sigmar tilted his head as he focused on the boy, unsure of what to do next. Holding up a wet rag, he gently wiped streaks of dirt from the boy's vacant face.

"What…could've happened?" asked Ketil, his expression agitated. "The animals are missin' from the barn, and there's nothing else alive—not even a chicken—on the whole farm."

Chewing on his lip, Sigmar didn't answer immediately. Instead, he looked over to his bag and thought for a moment. Walking over to it, he rummaged through his pack and fetched a small pouch and some water from two interior pockets. Pulling out a handful of salted jerky, he held it next to the boy's face.

Magnus took the food and absently began chewing on it, but his thoughts were still somewhere else, lost in the trauma of whatever happened to him. Sigmar followed it up with the flask of water, and the child drank from it without complaint.

Stepping out of the earshot of the boy, Sigmar pulled Ketil close and whispered in a serious, almost panicked tone. "I don't know what happened to Halfden and his wife. There seems enough blood for them, if they were completely drained of it. About the young girl, I…"

Ketil had never seen Sigmar disturbed this way, and he put his hand on his friend's shoulder as Sigmar's words drifted off. It was the only sign of comfort a gruff man such as he would ever offer, and it seemed enough to bring Sigmar back from his fearful thoughts.

Taking a mind-focusing breath, Sigmar snapped out of it and returned to the present. After a few moments of silence, he paced back to his bag. He began stuffing things inside from the family table, including the broken cross and some plates that had littered the kitchen floor.

"We better get back," said Sigmar, his expression now focused and controlled. "The priest is gonna want to see this.

Whoever did this needs to be found. I get the feelin' we're gonna need help, and I'm not coming back this way without it."

Pulling the pack over his shoulder, Sigmar went to the boy and lifted him from his seat. Magnus' slight frame, swaddled in Ketil's fluffy cloak, seemed to melt into Sigmar's powerful embrace, and he let himself be carried to the door, his eyes still blank and unbothered.

Looking back to Ketil, Sigmar waited for his companion to open the door. Moving quickly to help, Ketil rushed to the door and pulled it open. Unmoving, Sigmar frowned at him, his eyes bulging in silent request for Ketil to do something else.

Catching himself, Ketil unsheathed his sword before stepping outside. Panning his gaze around to act as protector for Sigmar and his precious cargo, he waved them toward the waiting horses. As the group hurried forward, the howling wind around them picked up, and with worried eyes, the men rushed to depart the now-deserted farm.

# Chapter Seven

Kristian sat in the dimly lit main room, perched at a small table, and stared down at several weathered parchments. Visibly frustrated, he ran his hands through his greasy dark hair, then mocked his own perceived stupidity by banging his forehead several times with a cupped hand.

Breathing deep, Kristian took his time to gently shuffle through the crinkled sheaves, staring at columns of scribbled numbers while he pondered some important task. His expression was a mix of flustered child and lost adult, as if the questions he contemplated were a riddle meant to expose his unbending ignorance of the all-knowing world.

The room around him was lit by two lamps hanging from posts that supported the sagging roof, while three blurry glass windows on the walls showed darkness encroaching from the descending night outside. A dark-stone fireplace at the back of the room contained a steady fire, its licking flames heating the room and providing further illumination to the cozy and attractive interior of the structure.

A kitchen area to the back of the space was occupied by Erik, who leaned near a large pot and stirred a bubbling stew in a cooking pot suspended over hot embers. His face was like that of a proud parent as he gazed down admiringly at the fragrant concoction of broth, meat, and potatoes. The stew's delicious aroma drifted up and about the home, infusing the area with a pleasant atmosphere.

Outside, the wail from the never-ending northerly wind pierced through the exterior log walls of the place, its shrieking whoosh barely audible over the crackling blaze of the blackened old hearth inside. The faint sound of the rushing wind lent a sense of isolation to the comfortable home, as if the room was a contained boat floating in a lost and dark ocean of distant screams.

A heavy metal-and-wood crucifix hung over the main door, and a set of durable cabinets lined one wall, showing well-kept wooden bowls and plates in four neatly aligned stacks. To their side were several ladles and assorted eating utensils, including a clean butcher knife and tongs for handling hot items.

Spaced evenly between the exterior walls in the middle of the large room was another tidy hand-hewn table, surrounded by bulky benches padded with shaggy furs. In a display area on a nearby shelf were numerous hand-carved ivory figurines of arctic foxes and harbor seals, both animals that predominated in the local area. The carved animal renditions were appealing and precise, as if their sculptor had used great skill and countless hours to lovingly craft them from tusks of the type of walrus inhabiting the arctic sea to the north of the Eastern Settlement.

Grunting in annoyance, Kristian grabbed a quill from its holder and dipped it into an inkwell. Mumbling numbers to himself, he scrawled some figures on the paper, then worked through the columns of math with an aggravated tapping of his foot on the hard earthen ground.

Setting the quill aside, Kristian buried his face in his hands, and it appeared he wanted to scratch his eyes out from the failed accounting endeavor. Whatever the content of his work, he clearly didn't entirely grasp what he was doing.

Striding from the simple kitchen, Erik approached the table. With a patient smile on his face, he pointed down to paperwork, letting a smile cross his understanding features. "It will take time, but you'll get used to it. Took me a decade to understand the numbers in business."

Stepping closer, Erik reached down and arranged the papers in careful order, making sure the pages were properly aligned. "Just pay attention to the inputs. Make sure the price you offer accounts for your labor, no matter how much the customer says otherwise. Nobody, especially us, can afford to work for free."

Sighing, Kristian took his hands from his face and stared up at his father. "Why don't other men have to learn this? I'm the only one in the village that has to do math and write?"

"Because..." replied Erik, and he pointed down to the parchment with a thoughtful look. "Other men are happy to work for others all their lives. There's nothing wrong with that. We all have our parts to play in the world, and it's understandable to not take on the responsibility of running things ourselves."

Erik walked back to the kitchen, where he bent down and ladled stew into a clean bowl. Moving to a crude wood-fired oven, he grabbed a crust of fresh bread from its top and returned to his son. He set the meal in front of Kristian, and Erik's eyes considered his next words carefully. "But you gotta to learn to be your own man. Provide for yourself...and a family...someday."

The room was silent for a while, with Erik pondering their near future while Kristian frowned. The truth of living a remote life meant that marriage and having children were not something to be waited on for too long a time. Instead, starting a family was something to be embraced at a young age, because in a society with a small population and little room for demographic error, prosperity could only be pursued with many helping hands and a nurturing familial environment.

Erik wasn't getting any younger, and he didn't much like the idea of growing into old age without a burgeoning family to help him. He realized that such thoughts were perhaps a bit selfish, but in an area and time when communal help was impossible to access, you had to at least try to plan for the future. Doing so meant pushing his son to hurry up and find a good woman to settle down with.

Kristian obviously understood the not-so-subtle suggestion, and he frowned as he worked through his own thoughts of family and love, even as he realized those things sometimes might not go hand-in-hand. Returning to his ledger of papers, Kristian looked more determined as he squinted down at his work.

Patting Kristian on the shoulder, Erik walked to the entry door, where he took his heavy woolen cloak from a peg on the wall. Pulling on the warm garment, he opened the door. Outside, the distant sound of wind grew to a pitch as the early night's rushing air moved into the relaxed home. Grimacing, Erik stepped into the forbidding night and let the door shut with a lonely bang.

With Kristian now alone, he studied for a few moments longer as he tried to push away his father's words. Growing bored, he pushed the work aside and looked about the room, gazing at the loving environment he had known all his life. He knew he was lucky to have such a place and a caring father, but other thoughts continually preyed on his mind, constantly ruining his concentration.

Reaching into an inner pocket, Kristian pulled out a white ribbon made of simple cloth. He stared at it awhile, a dreamy and sad expression washing over his face. Twisting it in his fingers, his mind drifted away as he played with the edges of the material. His eyes became distant and he focused elsewhere as memories flooded his thoughts, taking him into more enjoyable times from the past.

#

*A younger and contented Kristian sat in a hot springs pool surrounded by rocky outcroppings. Steam from the warm water drifted into the air, making his unclothed form barely visible in the morning light. Around him, the day was bright and appealing, with the clear sky illuminating a rocky field running down a slope to the shore of the open ocean.*

*In that calm sea were a series of glaciers, lazily floating by in the quiet background. The placid water of the ocean's surface was appealing and smooth, making the environment attractive and somehow perfect for this remote day.*

*Staring up, Kristian's dreamy gaze focused ahead. Approaching him from across the pool, the similarly younger and unclothed Sigri waded toward him. Her fierce and hungry gaze moved down to Kristian, eying him like a mischievous and hungry predator.*

*As her bare legs sloshed through the warm water, Kristian's disbelieving eyes moved down to take in her unseen naked form. Something like fear and ecstasy combined to make the rest of the world seep into an immaterial backdrop, and his youthful thoughts grew intense as his face flushed with helpless expectation.*

#

*Younger Kristian stood in a forest clearing, looking lanky and boyish as he stared intently ahead. Dressed in loose-fitting britches and wrapped in seal skins, he held up a wooden sword and peered into the misty woods. The overcast sky and fog made the area strangely gloomy, and visibility was difficult.*

*With a shout, he rushed forward, attacking the bark of a sturdy tree by slamming the practice weapon with hard strikes. The blows were authoritative and firm, and their thuds filled the quiet environment with an echoing finality as he rained abuse on the unmoving hardwood.*

*Breathing hard, Kristian stood back as he reflected on his fighting activity. Rubbing his arms, he flinched from the pain of the jolting slashes on the hard surface. His joints and muscles ached from the effort, with the residual ringing of the impacts still felt deep within his bones.*

*Letting the mock weapon fall to the ground, he flexed his hand to drive off the cramps from the raw exertion of practice. Feeling confident in his combat acumen, he peered to the side with a sly and appreciative grin.*

*Sigri stood there, watching him with an impressed smile. Moving close, her pleasant stare engaged Kristian's eyes as she took his pained hand into hers. Pulling his fingers near her chest, she took out a white ribbon and tied it around his fingers. As she intertwined his hand with her own, she completed the knot, making their digits bind together as one.*

*Looking up from the affectionate gesture, Kristian's innocent eyes focused on Sigri. His face glowed with youthful love, almost as if his soul was lit with its own light source.*

#

The clacking sound of a wooden tray being dropped on the table brought Kristian back to the present. The tray was laden with recently butchered meat, and fresh blood from the hunks of animal flesh pooled in places on its uneven surface.

Standing next to the table, Erik stared down at Kristian. Trying to control his strained voice, he gestured down to the blocks of flesh. "This is our last cow, and now we can't replace it. You know why?"

Kristian looked up, trying to reassert control over his drifting mind. Lost for words, he didn't meet his father's gaze. "You mean…because of the weather?"

Erik shook his head. "No, because we lost half our income from foraging and hunting. You know how that happened?"

Kristian didn't answer. Shame filled his features as he looked anywhere but at Erik.

"Because of your obsession with that…girl," said Erik, his face growing depressed. "Our one customer that paid in coin and on time is lost forever."

Taking a moment to collect himself, Erik breathed deep and lowered his tone. "Can you see how your actions affect others? Life is about controlling your emotions. You think she's worried about you right now?"

Kristian dropped his eyes to the table, tracing imaginary pictures on its surface with his trembling fingers.

"No," continued Erik, and he lowered his face to his son, tipping Kristian's chin toward him with his callused fingers. In response, Erik finally met his father's eyes, though he stayed silent.

Erik lowered his voice, but some bitterness leaked into his words. "She's counting her wealth with that rich bastard of a husband, while we get to worry about having enough to eat this winter."

Picking up the white ribbon, Erik waved it in front of his son, and his voice grew imploring, almost to the point of begging. "You've got to let it go and focus on your…our…lives. I can't do it all alone."

For a moment there was silence, and Erik took a moment to compose himself. He could see that Kristian understood the truth of what he said but understanding and acting on it were two very different actions.

When he was a teen, Erik had quickly grasped what he needed to do in life, but Kristian had always had a slower time learning about the world. It might have been due to his mom's death when he had yet to turn ten, but being stuck in a world where you dreamed instead of acted was not something Erik understood well. He was at a loss to empathize with the boy, even if he loved him completely.

From the door, a sharp knock came. Surprised by the interruption, both Erik and Kristian were confused as they considered who would be visiting them—at this time of night travel was hazardous and unwise. Motioning for Kristian to grab his scabbarded weapon from a hook on a nearby post, Erik snatched his own sword from the other table and carefully approached the door.

When Erik eased open the door, Iqiak stared back at him, his form barely identifiable from the darkness outside. As he leaned into the faint light of the interior lamps, Iqiak's face was tired and gravely serious. Glancing back and forth, he moved his attention between father and son.

"Do I interrupt?" asked Iqiak, sounding hesitant.

Shocked, Erik met the gaze of his friend. After a moment, he shook his head in an attempt at being polite. Offering a sincere smile, he motioned Iqiak inside.

#

The house shone with minimal light from its dim oil lamps, and Iqiak's bulky animal skins were hung against the front wall near his propped hunting spear. The items were arranged to allow quick access, as if he intended to not overstay his welcome and be ready to leave at a moment's notice. In the back of the room, the fire crackled from the fireplace, its gentle smoke rising to exit a conical venting hole in the Norse ceiling.

In the middle of the communal area, Iqiak, Kristian, and Erik sat hunched over the larger table. Several bowls of tasty stew and chunks of fragrant bread occupied most of the space on the table's surface, and Iqiak slurped loudly as he spooned delectable portions into his eager mouth. For a considerable time, the Inuit man grunted and gulped down the food as his hosts watched, their faces happy that he could so enjoy the hearty meal.

Finally finishing the thick soup, Iqiak leaned back and sighed contentedly. Using a final hunk of bread, he sopped up the remains of the broth before popping it into his mouth. Extending his cup to Kristian, he received from a ceramic mug a final splash of Erik's best home brew and quaffed the drink with an appreciative grin.

Leaning back, Iqiak's formerly serious and disquieted expression was replaced with that of a man momentarily gratified by his full belly. There was nothing like a robust meal to drive away the rigors of travel in this remote environment, and all three men were aware that the hospitality of a good meal was an intrinsic and welcome aspect of both of their cultures.

Erik was accustomed to the Inuit habit of not immediately talking about matters while enjoying a host's generosity; such was the way of their lifestyle and traditions that news, even important and urgent information, needed to be meted out in digestible bits, so that facts could be taken in and processed with due wisdom and contemplative thought.

Iqiak's ancestors had survived in the ice and snow for thousands of years, and such an accomplishment was only possible with people that weighed their decisions carefully. Rashness often brought undesired outcomes, up to and including the most deadly results.

But still, there were times to just get on with it, and Erik decided to suspend the formalities for now. "You haven't been here for several months, and you always try to let me know when you're comin'? What's bothering you?"

Iqiak didn't seem to be disappointed by Erik's rush to get to the point, and he nodded in agreement to the hurried conversation. "It is very bad. We found where our hunter was, but his body not there. He killed large bear, but his own blood also there. Nothing else, like he become ghost."

"Maybe another bear got him?" asked Kristian, leaning forward and scrunching up his features in confusion. "There are more than a few out there."

Iqiak smiled grimly and shook his head. "No, Kristian. No other tracks from another bear. No tracks at all."

Erik nodded as he thought through Iqiak's words. Showing deliberative respect for the lost Inuit hunter, he was nevertheless curious as he met Iqiak's gaze in the dim light.

"It's a hard life out there, even for your people," Erik said, keeping his words controlled and deferential. "There's all sorts of dangers on the ice, but if not a bear, what could it be?"

Iqiak was quiet for some time, wanting to talk but apparently reluctant to reveal what he knew. As Erik became more concerned with his friend's reticence to clarify his thoughts, Iqiak finally leaned forward and spoke in a soft voice, like he dreaded that his words would be overheard.

"Something much worse," whispered Iqiak. "Something that can destroy everyone. I already contact my people and will tell other tribes even farther away, but first, I come to you. To warn you…and I hope you all listen."

With that, Iqiak leaned back again, going quiet as he studied the faces of his friends. The room remained silent as Kristian and Erik returned his gaze, their demeanors growing increasingly worried.

#

Dry wind blew across the barren expanse of arid tundra. Outcroppings of frost-covered rocks and broken ice lay in the distance, and gloomy light leaked through puffy streaks of clouds in the late afternoon haze.

Towards the west, a smooth field of ice stretched toward the shoreline of the arctic sea. Where the choppy waves of the ocean met the snowy shoreline, an igloo stood only a dozen yards from the frigid water, looking like an icy outpost in the lonely and intimidating terrain.

Surrounding the igloo was a multitude of various skins stretched on posts in the cold air, with hunks of animal blubber and flesh hung to dry in the brisk wind sweeping across the open fields around it.

A large rack carved of weathered driftwood was erected between the igloo and the sea. On it were scores of fish that were spiked in intervals on sharp notches. Set there to dry, the husks of the varied char and sea trout were spaced neatly, and their number was plentiful enough to provide extensive food stores of dried fish for whomever lived inside.

Inside the igloo, furry bear skins lined the snowy floor, and tough hides of walruses and seals were hung at intervals along the icy walls to help keep warmth inside. Several spears were bunched in easy reach to the side amongst various crude bags and personal possessions.

An improvised short table made of more driftwood was set in the middle of the hut, and a family of three Inuit sat cross-legged around it. The family was comfortable and untroubled as they picked at various fish that were splayed out on the crude table before them. They munched from the delectable catch of large fish, stripping off bits of flesh as they chewed on the oily and uncooked morsels.

Tonraq, the father, was not yet old, but his leathery skin was typical for a people that were exposed to the harsh element of icy wind and the intense glare of the ice in the far north.

He sat across from his wife, Yura, and his daughter, Nunik. The remarkable features of the females were alive in the confines of the dimly lit ice hut, and the women munched contentedly as they returned Tonraq's affectionate gaze.

"The winter comes earlier, as it has for some time," said Tonraq, his cadenced tone reflecting neither concern nor surprise. "We will have to move farther to sea, I think, to hunt more before the harsher weather comes. I will move south to notify my brother, and he will bring the canoes."

Between chews of her filleted meal, Nunik smiled across at her father, flashing a playful grin. "Will he brink Tulok for the first harvest? I will keep him company as he scouts the route for our first expedition."

Tonraq raised an eyebrow at his daughter, letting a partial frown turn his lips down as he considered her words. His measured response was mildly disapproving, though not angry. "Tulok is promised to another family, daughter, which you already know. You should only fish where you are allowed to keep the catch for yourself."

Yura's mischievous giggle joined the conversation, and the smiling mother inclined her head toward the igloo's entry with a similarly naughty grin. "If you had only fished where you were allowed, husband, I would be partnered with your cousin. A good hunter makes her own luck."

Nunik nodded at her mother, slightly raising her voice in a show of pride. "And I have always found the best fish, since the first days you taught me the ways of the sea and ice. I will catch the healthy prey I am destined for, not the rotten bits that fall from the rack."

Tonraq thought for a bit on the wisdom of his family, squinting his brow in frustration. After a moment of consideration, he grinned reluctantly and leaned back. Focusing on his family in the vague light, he realized his input was unneeded and unwanted, so he opted for silence as they smiled at him.

The igloo was quiet for a time as the noisy feast continued. Each fish carcass was stripped to the last bone, with nothing left to waste after being picked clean by their nimble fingers. The atmosphere was pleasant, and only a slight howl of the outside wind seeped into the narrow opening of the humble hut.

Abruptly, Tonraq canted his head to the side, as if some perplexing and unheard interruption from afar had disturbed his methodical eating. His gaze moved to the entrance as he searched for the source of this sudden disruption. Something was just out of place, and his eyes expressed confusion as he considered their surroundings.

"Husband, what is wrong?" asked Yura, her pleasant mood melting into concern as she searched Tonraq's face.

The family went quiet, letting the sound of even their own chewing die down as they waited to hear what was amiss. The air was full of expectation, even as no response came to their anxious ears.

Tonraq reached over to their stack of weapons, plucking a particularly fearsome-looking barbed spear from the pile of hunting implements. He allowed a mirthful smile to cross his face, trying to calm his family, but there was something in his features that betrayed real concern.

Tonraq was a man who was an expert on this environment and the hazards it contained, and the fact that he noticed something out of place was not lost on Yura and Nunik. They trusted his instincts completely, even if they themselves could not pinpoint what bothered him. Their eyes flitted about, looking for reassurance or explanation.

Leaning forward, Tonraq whispered to his wife with a broad and forced grin. "Maybe it is a long-lost woman that still searches for her perfect catch. I should not disappoint her."

Chuckling, Tonraq moved to exit the igloo, scooting through the opening and pushing aside the heavy curtain that blocked the way. Assuming a less concerned expression, Yura playfully smacked him on his way out.

When Tonraq departed, Nunik and Yura returned to their meal, recommencing their slurping consumption of the raw flesh. Several minutes passed, and mother and daughter remained quiet as they concentrated on finishing their food.

Abruptly, a strange THUNK was heard from outside, a sound that wasn't easily identifiable and had an unnerving quality to it. Gulping, Nunik looked to her mom with a worried frown as she raised her voice. "Father…is anything wrong?"

No reply came from Tonraq. Only the continuing shriek of the low wind on the open steppe answered her question.

Pointing to the spears, Yura grabbed one and faced the entrance. Taking up another, Nunik turned the same way while scooting to her mother's side. From outside, another odd sound emerged, a strange *schuking,* like that of a knife being sharpened on a leather strip.

Yura spoke in a trembling voice that rose to a desperate shout. "Tonraq, what…is happening?"

Still there was no reply. After a few moments, Yura set her jaw defiantly and squeezed outside through the opening. Nunik followed her, scared but determined as her eyes adjusted to the brighter backdrop of the waning day.

Emerging from the hut, the glow of sunlight still illuminated the area, but Nunik and her mother stared outwardly in surprise. A strange mist had encircled their camp, blotting out visibility and preventing them from seeing much of anything. A wall of fog made the world stop but a few meters from where they stood. In the wide scenery they had always known, full of endless seas and ice, now there were only the inky-white outlines of a dense cloud.

Both women held out their spears, warily facing towards what they could only feel, not see. Even the wind's perpetual whine seemed to have disappeared from this closed-off environment.

Yura crept cautiously to the side, and ahead of her loomed the outlines of the fish rack. There, she could see the profile of Tonraq against the rickety structure, standing up and very still. Breathing deep, she was relieved as she approached the wispy form of her husband in the roiling fog.

Except, he wasn't really standing. His arms seemed to hold himself up awkwardly. Something was terribly off with his silhouette.

Getting closer, Yura saw the horrid truth. Tonraq's arms were lanced on the sharp points used to suspend the fish. Facing away from his wife and daughter, he was impaled on his own spear, leaning forward and down on it, yet suspended strangely on its sharp edge. The gory point of the weapon had slightly emerged from his back, and all manner of his entrails and blood were splashed on the ground in front of him.

Yura screamed in fright and uncontrolled anguish. "Aiiyahh…no, Tonraq…no!"

Responding to her mother's despondent wail, Nunik ran to Yura's side, thrusting out her weapon defensively as her eyes focused on her father. They both stood in shock as they took in the horrific and ghastly sight, each struggling and unable to process what they were seeing.

From the edge of the mist, the Keelut encircled them, staying just out of their reach as its blurry outline moved in a predatory arc. Spinning around, both women tried to fend it off, even as they couldn't quite make out what hunted them. Trying to protect themselves, they turned back-to-back in a tight circle, facing out as they searched for Tonraq's killer. There was no sound from the fog, but they could sense their hunter was stalking them, ready to pounce from its depths.

Catching her breath and breathing in rasps, Yura motioned around them and yelled to Nunik, getting her attention with a suddenly forceful and strangely controlled voice. "Go to your uncle. Run, don't look back or stop. I will see you in the afterlife…with your father."

Without waiting for a reply, Yura waded away from her daughter, focusing on the blur of the Keelut in the dense mist.

Swinging wildly and stabbing ahead, she was quickly lost to Nunik, swallowed completely by the fog.

Taking a ragged breath into her fear-stricken lungs, Nunik lurched the other way, picking up speed as her stumbling legs carried her away from their home. Focusing into the swirling cloud, her terrified eyes searched for escape from their unknown attacker.

# Chapter Eight

The dining area was clean, and a large and polished wooden table stood at its center. The walls around were neat and kempt, with pleasant paintings of fjords and distant mountains providing a striking artistic appearance. Daylight flooded through open curtains around large windows along the exterior wall, its rays highlighting dust particles that floated in the spotless room.

Wrinkling her nose, Sigri stared down in annoyance. Standing near the end of the table, she focused on a luxurious tablecloth with various silverware and dishes laid carefully out on it. The maid watched obediently from behind her, her fingers interlaced in worried expectation while she awaited instructions.

"Why would anyone use four spoons?" asked Sigri, and she panned her gaze back to the maid, then over to the room's main entryway, where Rand watched his daughter with a controlled smile.

Rand chuckled at the question and moved closer to the table. He held a parchment in his hand, which he squinted at to read as he approached the table. "It says each has their own function: one is for soup, one is for mixing cream, one is for—,"

"One is for scooping out my eyes, I fear," interrupted Sigri, and she sat down on one of the chairs, ruffling her pretty but too-fluffy blue dress in the process. Sighing, she continued. "I thought people here were the same as in Iceland. Why the difference, with such…odd ways?"

Setting aside the etiquette instruction paper, Rand motioned politely to the maid, who bowed and exited the room. Speaking in a low voice, he adopted a considered tone, showing a reflective expression as he looked down at Sigri. "I think it has more to do with a person's station in life. I expect that those of limited wealth do not use so many utensils to eat, just like everyone here."

Taking some time to think, Rand paced to the window and looked out, where his gaze fell on green fields covered in frost that had yet to be melted with the day's heat. His smile faded as he considered the ever-colder weather, like he had allowed the chill from outside to also freeze his good thoughts for the day.

Turning back to Sigri, Rand's tone was academic as he wrestled with a distant memory. He arched an eyebrow, ready to impart some appreciation of the wider world to his sheltered daughter. "I've read the world is a fascinating place. From one country to another, people speak different languages, eat different foods, and even worship the Lord differently…"

Rand's words died away as Sigri, disinterested and deep in thought, clasped her hands on the table, picking at her recently cleaned and buffed fingernails.

"I like the way we do things, father."

Looking doubtful, Rand stepped near Sigri and patted her on the shoulder in a sign of support. His expression showed a cross between an expectant father and a pretending friend.

The gesture was forced, and with a sour grimace, Sigri shrugged off his touch. Standing, she spoke in a low whisper. "He's a good man, but I'm not sure I would have agreed to this marriage if I had known it would turn out like this. Wealth alone does not make life worth living."

Rand crinkled his face up at such a revelation, clearly disagreeing with the sentiment. But he still stayed silent, choosing to avoid confrontation over such financial heresy.

After a moment, Sigri inhaled a deep and dissatisfied breath. Grinding her teeth, she walked past her father and exited the room without waiting for him to follow. Rand scowled at the disrespectful gesture and followed her out.

Pacing outside through a side door, Sigri came to stop on a landing, where her view of the surrounding area was expansive. She placed her hands on the hand-carved railing, then alternated her gaze between the roiling ocean and the murky forest that ran up to it.

The sky was overcast, but the day had not lost its probing light, and several footpaths into the forest were easily visible. It was a view the entire settlement envied, but here she was, unhappy and questioning where life had now taken her.

Below and to the side, a groundskeeper struck the ground with a pick, trying to enlarge a ditch in the frozen earth to increase the flow of drainage on the property. Seeing Sigri, the sweat-streaked worker stopped his efforts and removed a floppy hat to bow her way. Sigri gave him a polite and considerate nod, recognizing him as the father of a girl she had known well throughout her youth.

Nodding again, the man returned to his work.

Rand strode out of the house, looking impatient as he cleared his throat to get Sigri's attention. When they met gazes, both became silent as each contemplated her worries about her new life, but for very different reasons: Rand focused on his prospective happiness and material comfort, while Sigri dreaded the prospect of a loveless future far from what she considered home.

From a window far to the back of the estate, Thorstein noticed his wife and father-in-law through the window of his study. Reading a parchment with the light from the window, he lowered the paper and focused on the pair. His gaze grew fierce as he fixed his eyes on them. Unable to hear their words, he was nevertheless interested in the content of their conversation.

Speaking to not draw attention, Rand stepped close to Sigri. "You're lucky he chose you, Sigri, he could have had any—."

"Then why don't I feel lucky? I can't even say hi to my friend?" asked Sigri, cutting off her glowering father.

Rand's eyes opened to an angry stare, and he tilted his head in disapproval. "Your 'friend' was a young lover, and yes, I was aware of that. The indiscretions of youth have plagued us all. But, you can be certain Thorstein was also aware, and he's been very understanding up to this point."

There was silence for a moment, and Sigri pointedly did not deny the accusation. After a deep breath, she tried to change the direction of the conversation and softened her voice. "Father, it is not a chore for me to make a better life for us. I just don't want to give up everything we are and have always..."

Sigri trailed off and looked toward the forest. From a trail in the woods, a young boy broke free of the overgrowth and ran toward the estate. As he got closer, she could see he was one of the children employed by Father Galmand to facilitate church business. They were expecting no news from the priest, so this messenger's arrival was not a good sign. Sigri and Rand frowned in apprehension.

When the boy got close to the veranda, he stopped short and looked up at Rand and Sigri. Trying to catch his breath, he spoke in rasps as he pointed at Rand. "Father Galmand...asks you to come quickly...right away...and Mr. Olafsson."

As Sigri and Rand traded concerned glances, Thorstein emerged from the house. Hurrying toward their young guest, he looked worried at the sudden interruption. Nodding to his wife, his puzzled eyes focused on the messenger boy, hoping the young man might have more to say.

Instead, the boy stayed silent and continued his gasps for air. While the group exchanged noncommittal stares, the only sound was the laborer whacking away at the rocky ground on the field to their side.

#

Darkness covered the forest, preventing easy visibility through clusters of swaying branches that clogged the way forward on a faintly lit footpath. Throughout the nearby woods, a rustle from the relentless wind moved thickets of brush to either side of the trail, making a noisy and forbidding atmosphere in the chilly night air.

Thorstein strode fearlessly ahead, dodging twigs and low-hanging overgrowth as he plodded forward. Holding up a flickering torch, he was determined as he focused on each turn in the frozen earth's twisting pathway. With each step, his stiff boots crunched in the soil, and his resolute gaze scoured the area in front while he ducked through the cluttered underbrush of the dark woods.

Behind him, Rand struggled to keep up, while also making sure to not catch a wayward branch in his face. Trying to focus on the light of Thorstein's fire, his demeanor was somewhat less determined; in fact, his eyes sought each new shadow as a potential ambush, and he moved his hand down defensively to the hilt of a long knife tucked into his leather belt.

Ahead, the forest parted, and a field opened up to the Hvalsey Church and the priest's residence that stood behind it. Stopping, Thorstein gazed around the moonlit clearing expectantly, like someone should have been waiting for him. For a moment he stood there, taking in the shadowy sight of the lonely church and house as he thought out his next move.

Seeing the fields empty and the church dark, Thorstein focused on the humble home of the pastor, which was illuminated from within with light from several cloudy windows on its side wall. The squat building was not exactly welcoming, but it was the only place where their invitation from Galmand could reasonably be consummated with a visit.

Breathing deep, Thorstein set out across the land that had recently been abandoned of crops and livestock. He stepped through an open gate and passed by iced-over water troughs as he trudged toward Galmand's house. Behind, Rand continued his slower place and cautious visual investigation of their surroundings, as if some predator could be awaiting them from someplace in the open fields to the side.

Approaching the door of the residence, Thorstein rapped the thick wood and called out in an impatient tone. "We are here, Father Galmand. What do you need of us at this late hour?"

From the other side of the door was some rustling, followed by the clack of a lock being disengaged. When the door was pulled open, Erik stared out at Thorstein, and neither appeared happy for the renewed opportunity to chat. Their eyes met in the eternal lock of two people that have decided they will never be friends, and that unwritten but mutual contract was signed with the sour stare of each man's hostile gaze.

Scowling, Thorstein pushed past Erik and into the front room of Galmand's house, the same location where they had investigated the corpse of the priest from the Western Settlement a few days before. Standing in the lamplight farther in the room were Kristian, Galmand, Ketil, Sigmar, and Iqiak.

As Rand came in behind Thorstein, all eight of the men crowded the confines of the austere room. The table, taking up space at its center, made the throng of people close and uncomfortable, with little room to move about.

Strangely, everyone remained silent for some time, with each already-present man looking intently at the newcomers with worried eyes. It wasn't exactly fear that clouded their expressions, but instead a combination of dread and exasperation. Sigmar licked his lips awkwardly, while Ketil tugged at his beard with a sullen demeanor.

Finally growing tired of the silence, Thorstein spoke up, trying to put some authority into his voice. "What in Christ's name is going on?"

#

Shocked, Thorstein scanned the room, where he took in the features of each of the serious-minded men sitting around him. Ketil and Sigmar looked back with aloof indifference, while

Galmand and Rand awaited Thorstein's input with respectful and expectant faces.

Peering at him from directly across the table, Erik fixed Thorstein with an irritated expression but refrained from any interaction, while to his side, Kristian avoided the merchant's gaze entirely, seemingly eager to be anyplace else at the moment.

Sitting in the main room in Galmand's house, Thorstein grimaced as he processed the situation, like he was waiting for the punch line to a bad joke. When none came, he chewed on his lip, trying to focus his thoughts to work through the reasoning for what he had just heard.

Iqiak stood with crossed arms to the side, the only person present who was not seated. The Inuit hunter watched the group with acute interest. His eyes flitted from one man to another, gauging the character and bearing of each individual in the assembled party. With a serious and unmoving frown on his face, he waited for an important conversation to develop around what he had already revealed.

Thorstein pushed himself back from the table and stood. Stretching his back and looking about, he adopted a contemplative train of thought, wondering if this whole business could somehow be set right, like the ledgers in some complicated transaction that just needed a smarter accountant's eye to get the balances in proper order.

"We have a dead priest and a missing family," said Thorstein, finally starting the conversation. "And we also have some Inuit that are missing, a fact that is known to happen in the wilds of this…difficult land."

Ketil tugged at his beard in response, and his raspy voice was grave as he droned his words out in response. "A family that was bled out in their own house. And…the child who was there said it was the devil that did it."

"That could mean many things to a child," replied Thorstein. "A bandit or some marauders could seem like a devil to a child—"

"The boy didn't say 'a devil', he said 'the devil'," said Erik, interrupting Thorstein with a scowl. "It just might be a difference in wording we should pay attention to."

Thorstein gave Erik a sour look but agreed with a restrained nod to his logic. He paused to collect his thoughts before continuing. "My point is just that when a child sees something horrible, it does not mean it should be taken literally. The view of the young does not often match with reality. It does not mean we are dealing with…real devils."

There was silence for a moment, and the group members pondered to themselves the recent events and what they could mean. The sense of disquiet was palpable, and with no answers forthcoming, the prospects for solving what was happening did not look to be getting better any time soon.

Sitting back on his chair, Galmand shook his head and sighed. He pointed to the busted crucifix on the table—the one collected from the farm, where the boy had been retrieved.

"Perhaps you are right, Thorstein, perhaps these are just the mumblings of a scared and traumatized boy. But what brigand steals corpses and destroys the crosses of our Lord?"

More quiet followed, and when no more ideas were spoken, Iqiak uncrossed his arms and stepped near the table. The room as one focused on him, like they had forgotten he was there.

"We are people of ice and sea. We live where you only travel," said Iqiak, moving his gaze between the Norsemen. "We know North since man first created by Big Spirit. We understand dangers we face. But this not the work of man, it is work of great evil."

Disbelieving stares were shared amongst the party, but Erik slapped the table and pointed to Iqiak with a nod. His words were convincing as he implored the other men to listen. "I trust this man with my life. Nobody knows more about the cold outlands than him. Nobody."

Galmand nodded, glancing toward Iqiak with approval. But he was still dubious. "We appreciate that, Erik. I, for one, have always admired our Inuit friends, even though there are differences in what and who we follow."

Standing slowly, Galmand moved over to Iqiak, stopping on the way to shake out the pain in his gouty leg. Getting close to the Inuit, he placed a reassuring hand on his shoulder, then turned to the others.

"It is apparent something dreadful is transpiring in our peaceful settlement," said Galmand, invoking his priestly and wise voice. "But what do these killings have to do with some demonic threat? The Good Lord sees fit to test us at times, but I do not know of a place when he has done so with something otherworldly. There is enough evil in the heart of man to challenge us. Real demons are unnecessary."

Nodding amicably to Galmand in response, Iqiak moved to a vantage point where everyone could see him. Raising his arms, he lowered his hands in a mollifying gesture. "I will tell story, then I leave you to decide for yourself. I only come here to warn, not demand."

The room became quiet as Iqiak drifted into his inner thoughts, perusing his memory for the right words in a language he had never fully mastered. "My people live on snow for a hundred lives. We do not write our story, but we pass down our heritage with words. We make sure to get every word correct, because it is only way to understand clear history."

Iqiak gestured out one of the windows. "We take from the land and sea what we need to live, and we move to new places that have a bounty for our people, to get more food. It is a good life we lead until we get to meet our fathers in your 'heaven.'"

Iqiak stopped for a moment, and after a friendly nod from Galmand, continued. "But, it told by our wise men of times when area is warmer…like it has been up until recent times. When a 'demon' as you say, emerges from darkness to steal from the living. This demon steal the good from people to use for its own purpose."

Thorstein rolled his eyes and shook his head as if to say, *how could these people believe such nonsense? Are we not people of reason?*

Iqiak ignored him and proceeded with his story. "'This 'Keelut,' this evil thing, will first attack men that are shaman, men who follow Great Spirit."

"Like father Sturlesson, from the Western Settlement?" asked Erik.

"Yes, and two of our priest men. Shamans," responded Iqiak. "They also are missing. It is said that the Keelut will feed on their insides for power. To grow stronger."

Looking uncomfortable, Galmand gulped and ground his jaw at this new and disturbing information. Several of the others glanced sympathetically at him, for the first time feeling sorry for their pastor in his chosen profession.

"But then, Keelut will feed on all who live in the cold area, until there are no more living," Iqiak said, keeping his features serious and flat. "It then returns to dark to wait for new, warmer time."

"To hibernate?" asked Kristian, interjecting his youthful voice into the discussion. The entire room was surprised at his unexpected suggestion, but Iqiak nodded, impressed.

"Yes, Kristian," said Iqiak. "Until area warms again, until new men return to the Keelut's area. Then it comes again…in same cycle."

Thorstein tilted his head in unhidden disbelief. "Then why hasn't it come until now? The Norse have been here for four hundred years. Now, this demon wants to destroy us? Why would such a thing wait?"

Iqiak smiled without humor, shaking his head and looking into Thorstein's doubting face. "I do not know all about Keelut. Perhaps it waits until very end of warm time to become hunter. Perhaps time in its world is very different. I only know it is here now."

Galmand cleared his throat to deflect Thorstein's skepticism. "How have your people survived this 'Keelut' in the past?"

"We move," Iqiak said. "For many days of travel we move away from it—where Keelut not find us. It is not just my people. In any place where man try to live in cold, he will face this evil thing, when weather is warm. It is only matter of time."

Stroking his wispy goatee, Thorstein chuckled out loud. "So, you are saying that all people here…and in the other settlement…will have to leave? That we will be killed by some devil from a child's dream? You cannot be serious."

Iqiak nodded without hesitation, keeping his voice steady and plaintively avoiding Thorstein's disrespectful tone. "Yes, or you could come with us. Adopt our ways. Combine tribes. But to stay here is to die."

Thorstein grinned a fake smile to Iqiak, then moved his gaze to the rest of the room, looking expectantly to the others for confirmation of the insanity in the Inuit's words. One by one, he inquired in their eyes for a logical escape from this unbelievable predicament, as if merely not believing it would make the reality go away.

But no amusement or similarly doubtful expressions met Thorstein's stare. Instead, there came only the worried frowns of men facing a horrific threat they couldn't yet understand.

#

The darkness in the cavern was absolute. The stark nature of its blackness precluded normal sight, offering an obscured view into the pure nothingness that only exists in areas devoid of connection with the natural world and its various sources of light.

From that exquisitely dark void, a distant, rippling hum began, and its melody was almost like a rush of an incoming wave—if it were heard underwater. This strange sound seemed at first to be distant, and then grew into a more pronounced rush of fluid from deep inside the contained rock walls.

The cave of the Keelut then started to lighten, and its walls became visible under a hellish and red hue, one that glowed with the distant slushing of that strange watery chord emanating from deep within the earth. The flush of the sound grew in strength, and the walls continued to brighten under each escalation of its incoming sound.

As the extensive cave became dimly visible, the cauldron where the Keelut had earlier dropped human organs came into view. There was now no fire below it, and only calm and dark liquid resided within its mucky confines.

When the sloshing sound of liquid finally peaked into a constant state, a different and odd sight became evident on the slippery rocks to the side of the huge pot. Three large openings in the rock face were now evident in the slick stones of the wall next to the cauldron. The spots of these openings consisted of an inky breach of dense material, which roiled, as if flowing with some unnamable and obscuring solution. Nothing was visible beyond the surface of the strange openings.

From the earth around the area, a new, more organic sound gripped the cave. It was an indeterminate wail of voices, like some crowd from a distant point of geography was getting closer. Except, the voices were deep and shrill at the same time, as if their droning intensity were constant and didn't require breathing through vocal cords to make their manic utterances heard.

As the distant sounds grew stronger, they became identifiable as shrieks, but not the shrieks of anything human. Instead, they were the inhuman cries of something that only knew unending anger, pain, and torment—the cries of the forsaken.

Striding from the corner of rock formations in the back of the cave, the Keelut moved toward the slots. As it approached the breaks in the wall, the sounds from within grew in pitch, and the creature's bulging veins, intersected throughout its hideous gray flesh, began to pulse with the same red tinge of the walls.

The effect on the Keelut's putrid form was that it entirely became a part of what made up this inner core of the mountain, as if its attachment with the wails and liquid sounds was entirely interdependent. When it stepped closer to the bizarre voids in the rock, the shrieking from within the spots grew to a feverish pace.

The Keelut held out both of his light-skinned and muscular arms, and hanging from its clawed fingers were three items: one crucifix and two of the Inuit bone necklaces. Pressing the items forward to the gaps in the rock, there was a loud popping sound, and each of the religious jewelry was sucked into the dense voids.

Stepping back, the Keelut inclined its obscene and angular head, as if considering the result of its actions. Apparently satisfied, it moved away from the stone holes, pacing towards the pathway leading to the exit from the mountain.

As the Keelut walked away, the terrified moans from the breaches in the stone grew louder yet, as if something was coming closer to the opening. As the cacophonous and anguished wails grew, the entire complex pulsated in expectation, like the stony formations of the interior mountain had formed into its own life-force.

# Chapter Nine

Sitting in the confessional, Galmand was wrapped smartly in his priestly robes. The dark red color of his garments, interlaced with stitched representations of the Christian cross, was just visible in the faint light making its way through the screens surrounding the diminutive room. A silver crucifix with a shiny metal chain hung loosely on his chest.

Galmand looked up to the ceiling and crossed himself as if warding off some unseen and particularly wicked sin. "You must keep your heart pure, young Kristian. The Evil One thrives on our desires and lusts, making us part of his wanton disregard for our Lord's wishes. It is only through moderation and self-control that we can avoid the traps the Devil has laid for us."

From the other side of one of the screens, a shadow dipped its head, bowing submissively in the darkness beyond the flimsy portal.

Kristian's tentative voice whispered in response. "I…try, Father, but I don't understand what to do. I can't think of anything else…"Galmand rolled his eyes as Kristian went quiet. He shuffled a bit from his side of the segregated confessional, trying to get comfortable as he contemplated the rash emotions and difficult-to-repress hormones of youth. Frustrated, he raised his voice.

"Give your worries and sorrows to the Lord," said Galmand, forcing his words into a patient and kind offer of religious advice. "He will comfort you and give you courage as you confront your sins. You must trust him. You can trust your father, your friends, me, all of us who are inveterate sinners by nature. How much more should you trust the perfection that is Jesus Christ?"

There was silence in answer to Galmand, with Kristian squirming in shame behind the anonymizing screen in response.

Galmand took this as a cue to end the confession, and holding up a crucifix toward the shadowed form of Kristian, he spoke in a supportive and understanding voice. "Say three Hail Marys as penance. I absolve thee of thy sins. Go in peace, and sin no more."

Outside the small confessional, the church was empty except for a lone parishioner. Erik sat quietly in one of the pews, staring up at the large life-sized cross above the altar at the end of the small church. His eyes were fierce and watery as he focused them forward, lost in his personal thoughts of devotion and self-reflection.

It was at moments like this that Erik most missed his wife. She had been such a devout believer that prayer and holiness had seemed part of her innate nature, and she would not hesitate to show her displeasure if Erik was slow to attend mass or extol the virtues of a life spent according to the precepts of faith in God. It had been more than a decade since her passing, but every time he attended services at church, he half-expected to look over and see her peaceful expression bowed in quiet contemplation at his side.

Erik shook away the wave of pain that washed through his mind in response to her distant memory. He had long since come to peace with her death, and he realized he would have to wait a bit longer to see her in heaven. Still, if he was honest with himself, even though he believed in God and loved Him, the most important facet of the afterlife to him was to be reunited with his beloved wife, Maria.

Kristian exited the confessional and strode gently toward his father. He lowered himself next to Erik, clasping his hands in prayer and murmuring the words of his penance as he squinted his eyes shut. Lost in his thoughts, Kristian focused uniformly on overcoming his wants and weaknesses through prayer.

After several minutes of quiet, Erik seemed to awaken from his personal stupor. Blinking his eyes slowly, it was as if he was seeing the area for the first time when he emerged from his trance. Peering around self-consciously, he wiped his eyes, relieved that Kristian had not seen the errant tears making their way down his haggard cheeks.

Galmand emerged from his section of the confessional, and he looked over his church with a contented expression, like that of an endlessly proud father. He was surprised when his gaze found Erik, and even more so when Erik motioned him over with a respectful wave of his hand.

Ambling towards father and son, Galmand leaned down and smiled as he spoke to Erik in the low tone reserved for the interior of church. "Do you wish to offer your confession?"

Erik's mouth was dry as he responded, as if his throat had constricted while praying, making his tone crack in the calm and noiseless environment. "No…father. I was hoping…we could talk for a while."

Coming to his full height, Galmand cocked his head and considered the request as he stroked his beard absently. Nodding and keeping a polite face, he motioned his head towards the front of the church.

#

Outside, the day was bright, and the gentle wind offered a subtle hint of the cold that usually permeated the area. The ocean was brisk to the south, with its white-topped waves rolling far into the distance.

Galmand and Erik stood next to each other facing over the sea, enjoying the view in quiet consideration of the rough and dangerous beauty that surrounded them. Neither said anything for the moment, apparently contented to enjoy the waning day as Fall closed in around their church and village.

Behind them, Kristian dug through their cart, pulling free the weapons they had stored there while inside the church. Approaching his father, he stopped and held out the ancient Norse sword. Erik took it and slid the scabbarded weapon into his waistband, taking some time to affix it in proper order with several leather straps. Kristian returned to the cart while Erik cinched the knots expertly to keep the sword tied close and within easy reach.

When he had finished, Erik looked up and noticed Galmand's disappointed frown. It was evident the priest was not happy that such things were necessary so close to the church. Arming themselves after a trip to see him was not something that the pastor had ever experienced, and it went against his nature to witness it, however essential it had become to be cautious.

"Has the world become such a dangerous place?" asked Galmand, and his eyes also moved to take in the long knife in Kristian's waist. "Surely this will not be a continuous state of affairs?"

"I hope it isn't, Father," replied Erik, and he shrugged, then tapped the sword with his hand. "Between bandits and demons, maybe you should protect yourself, too?"

Galmand chuckled in response, indicating the area around them with his chubby arms. "If my hand is needed in combat, this land is truly in worse shape than you have ever imagined."

Erik smiled at the joke but was quiet for a while as he pondered something. Looking back toward the forest, he lowered his voice and leaned toward Galmand. "I wanted to know if you wanted me to bring a message to the Western Settlement next week? We are to visit there on our way back from Disko Bay after the seal hunt."

The humor drifted away from Galmand's features, and he nodded with serious eyes. "They will be terrified to hear their priest is…gone. Father Sturlesson was not jovial, but he was godly. Why is it that the Lord allows his most committed servants to pass from this world at such a young age?"

There was pained silence in response to the question, and Erik's eyes drifted to the graveyard near the forest, the place where his wife was laid to rest all those years ago. From this distance he could not see her grave precisely, but where it lay was one of the most certain things in his life, with Erik having visited it thousands of times over the years. He considered the cold ground in which her remains had long since become bones, and he shuddered to think that was all that remained of the warm body he had loved so dearly.

Galmand noticed Erik's sorrowful disposition, and he clapped him on the shoulder to lighten his mood. "And to answer my own question, we cannot know the mind of God. It is only through faith in Him that we can trust our own small fates in this world."

Erik let himself be comforted by this, if only a little, then readjusted his gaze to Galmand. "Well, if you want anything from our journey, just let me know."

"That is unnecessary, Erik. They won't need a message."

Confused, Erik tilted his head at the priest.

Galmand responded with a broad smile, but just a bit of worry was evident underneath his caring expression. "The flock at the other settlement is without a shepherd. I will be joining you for the trip. In the face of adversity, we must stand as one to offer what we can to help our fellow believers. Even a fat old priest must do his part until we can petition the church for a replacement."

Erik grinned at that sentiment, nodding at Galmand affectionately. He was surprised at the priest's courage, but he also suspected any replacements for the dead priest would be long in coming.

Shaking hands with Galmand, Erik moved back toward his waiting wagon and Kristian. Not looking back, he motioned for them to depart into the forest.

#

A cluttered assortment of goods lay about the dim warehouse. Casks of imported oil, slags of iron, and metal pots for cooking were stacked to one side, while the other half of the building overflowed with crates of animal skins, rope, and walrus tusks.

To the front of the area were several cages of birds, specifically the Greenland Falcon, a variety that was a highly prized predator bird in Mainland Europe and often housed in the personal menageries of kings and royalty. A worker walked from cage to cage, feeding generous portions of minced animal flesh to the quiet birds. Their black eyes scanned their surroundings while their sharp-hooked beaks pecked at the morsels.

In the middle of the chaotic scene was Thorstein, and he rushed about the area, fussing over the assorted materials with his harried workers.

"We shall have to load the newer vintage first, to prevent spoilage," Thorstein exclaimed, pointing to some barrels that had yet to be stacked properly. "I cannot imagine what possessed me to import that wine in the first place, there is nobody left here who can pay for it. But, it will still fetch a good price in Iceland."

A burly laborer nodded to his demand, then hurried over to comply.

From the front of the warehouse entered Sigri, who looked around with attentive eyes. Focusing on Thorstein, she strode back to him with a determined scowl. She carried some parchments in her hand, and from the perturbed look on her face, was intent on a rather serious conversation with her husband.

Stepping in front of Thorstein, Sigri stopped with a curt focus of her furrowed brow on the merchant. He had not seen her enter and so was surprised with the interruption. The look of open hostility in her features did not bode well for a pleasant exchange of ideas.

Slapping her papers into Thorstein's chest, Sigri glared up at him. "When were you going to tell me about this?"

Glancing down at the scribbled accounting documents, recognition crossed Thorstein's face, and he pleaded with his eyes for Sigri not to make a scene. Nearby, various workers pretended to ignore the burgeoning confrontation, and for a few moments, there were only the sounds of the rustling and stacking of supplies in the background to be heard.

"Can we discuss this elsewhere?" asked Thorstein, taking the parchments and gesturing out the front of the warehouse.

Sigri nodded and spun that way, not waiting for Thorstein to follow. Reluctantly, he trailed her out of the entrance and over to a shaded collection of trees, an area that offered some privacy. Unlike the current mood of the couple, the day around them was pleasant and the sun was plentiful under the blue sky.

Standing with arms crossed, Sigri waited for him to stop in front of her. She was dressed in a casual purple dress, one that was too formal for this working area, but she was clearly uninterested in formal conventions at the moment.

Pointing down at the papers Thorstein now held, Sigri spoke in barely contained rage. "Well, husband. Am I to stand here until judgment day, or will you talk?"

"I…planned to tell you," responded Thorstein, clearly flustered. "Soon, in fact."

"Do you think I can't read?" asked Sigri, irritation making her face red. "Your final bills of lading? You are closing your accounts here?"

Thorstein took a deep breath, steadying himself and finally overcoming his surprise. "It…appears to be the smart thing to do. For both of us."

Sigri stepped back, letting her voice rise as she gestured around them. "Smart? You're going to abandon Greenland, after making a fortune here? What kind of person would do that?"

"It is not incumbent on me to continue losing money here—just because I have had success in the past. I have told you before, the future—."

"This is my home, my people…my future," said Sigri, cutting him off. Breathing deep, she tried to calm herself. "You said we could make a home here, even if only for part of the year. You gave your word."

Thorstein stepped closer to Sigri, raising his own voice into a more assertive tone. "Have you noticed that there is a killer—or killers—in this area? Or that there is barely enough food for people to eat? How responsible of a man would I be to subject you to this?"

Thorstein tried taking her into his arms. Sigri, after briefly pushing him away, reluctantly accepted the hug.

"When things have calmed down, we can come back. When it's safer," Thorstein said, and his lowered voice and matter-of-fact delivery made the proposal seem like the only rational choice to make.

Looking up at him, Sigri was quiet for a time as she processed his plans. She let her gaze roam away from his, where she took in the bustling warehouse and the simple men that scurried around it doing her husband's work. Deciding something, she pulled free from his grasp.

"Next week, they go on the annual seal hunt," Sigri said, and an emotionless expression crossed her face. "So the villagers have enough to eat over the winter."

Stepping back, Sigri looked down the trail toward their home. Glancing around, she motioned to the warehouse. "I am going with them, to help. If you want to take your things and flee across the ocean, that's your choice."

Starting down the trail, she paced away with quick steps and a focused mind. Speaking back over her shoulder, she didn't wait for a response. "But you'll be doing it alone."

#

Four small row-type boats were beached on the open shoreline of dark-crusted dirt and rocks. Made in the typical Norse fashion, they were capable of skirting ice packs and clogged waterways. They had a place for a small sail in their interior, but they were not currently outfitted with one. The only power to be used for traveling would be by men using oars and sweat to skirt their way along the ocean's powerful currents.

On a ridge above the shore, the view of the ocean and its icy hunks floating at various points was breathtaking, with the sea's dreamy and tilting surface running into the distance of the broader North Atlantic Ocean. Unpopulated and raw, it teemed with all manner of fish and whales, providing an endless bounty—if one knew how to harness its spoils.

Several men rummaged around the boats, packing supplies into their narrow and shallow hulls. Kristian and Erik leaned over one craft, stacking different-sized bags into the hold of the smallest boat. Spears and harpoons lay on the floor, already wrapped for the remote hunt.

In and around the other boats were several men, including Ketil, Sigmar, Galmand, Rand, and Sigri. Along with other sturdy villagers, they focused intently on their tasks. Each knew the survival of the Settlement and their families for the winter was predicated on their successful endeavors in the upcoming seal-hunting expedition.

Hauling a bag of hard biscuits into their boat, Erik breathed hard from the effort. Gesturing to the ocean, he spoke between fatigued breaths to Kristian. "Two days to get there, if we hurry up. We need to stay off the sea as much as possible. We'll camp over at Black Meadows on the way."

"Why did they call it that," asked Kristian, and his face twisted in discomfort at the name. "Seems like a weird name for uninhabited coastline."

Erik sat down on his ass, taking a break from vigorous labor for the moment. "Iqiak says there was some battle there long ago, between the Inuit and some band of outlaws. They had white skin like us but were not Norse. It was before his time, but to hear him tell it, his tribe's fighters got massacred. Only a few were able to escape."

Kristian shook his head as he considered this information, but his expression softened when he grabbed onto some forgotten memory. "Bjorndal from the market says there used to be raiders from the south who sometimes visited the area. Said they were called 'Basques' and they hunted whales in the region with their big ships. Said they left the Norse alone, but they could've attacked Iqiak's people. Maybe it was them?"

"Don't know if I believe that," replied Erik, and he squinted out to the ocean, staring hard. It was as if he expected a fleet of whale hunting ships to emerge from the horizon, proving his doubts wrong. "But I guess you never know."

Kristian followed his gaze across the watery distance, then changed the subject. "Isn't there somewhere else to stop? Doesn't sound like a nice place to camp, especially at night."

"Don't think so. Not unless you want to sleep on ice. I admire Iqiak, but that doesn't mean I can live like they do. Sometimes, I think they have ice in their veins, not blood."

Thinking more about it, Erik grimaced at the thought of having to do any of this. The annual sea hunt had become more treacherous as the years went by, with increasing ice flows and choppier seas making the expedition perilous. Problem was, it was not just their lives that were endangered by the trek, but also that of their entire settlement if they should fail. Starvation at this point had become a real possibility with the failure of their pastoral lifestyle, and their position as a continuously thriving outpost at the edge of civilization was no longer assured.

Erik understood that the sagas told the Norse had settled Greenland at the end of the last millennium, about the year 985 AD. Shortly thereafter, they had moved to settle farther up the west coast of Greenland, where the Western Settlement currently stood. Intriguingly, within twenty years after that, the Norse had also made landfall to the far West, where it was claimed by some that China lay.

There, the settlements of Markland, Helluland, and Vinland were abandoned after only a short time, but it gave Erik and the other Norse of Greenland great pride to know that their ancestors had probed the edges of the known world more than four hundred years ago. Erik himself was one of only a few that had immigrated to this distant land recently, but these people were made of the same stock as he. This adopted land was his as well, and Erik cherished it for its endless beauty. Their pride was also his pride, and he felt entirely a part of this remote society.

The better times of the past were when the weather was warmer, though, when the sea routes to Greenland were not blocked by icebergs, and even grain was grown in their now fallow fields. It was also a time when diverse ships made port calls on a constant basis for trade, but now it was only Thorstein who did so.

Suddenly, Kristian cleared his throat and pointed up the hill, also tapping Erik on the shoulder to get his attention. Turning around, Erik stared at the path that descended from the top of the cresting ridgeline, where it ran down to where the boats were being loaded.

Descending the trail was Thorstein, and he was leading a horse being guided by two of his servants. Dressed in expensive clothes and with obviously too much gear to make the trip, he looked to be packed for an extensive vacation.

Erik and Kristian looked at each other, then over to Sigri in another of the boats. She was also processing the importance of her arriving husband, as well as the ridiculous amount of gear he planned to bring.

Wrinkling her brow, Sigri peered over to Erik and Kristian, contrasting her thoughts of happiness from Thorstein accompanying them with worry that his presence could get one or both of them killed. She knew Thorstein to be a respected and able merchant, but a hunter he was not.

As Erik, Kristian, and Sigri traded surprised glances, each of them frowned.

# Chapter Ten

That afternoon, the four small boats set out on their hazardous trip to harvest seals at Disko Bay. Aided by the coastal current that ran up the length of the iceberg-clogged western side of Greenland, they were nevertheless cautious as they rowed their way around huge shelves of ice and squat chunks of independent bergs on the ocean's surface. Huddled in their animal skins and wool clothing, the expedition members braced themselves against frigid arctic gusts as they forcefully drove their oars through the pristine water.

Far off to the left of the crafts, on the gray horizon that stretched into banks of murky clouds, the humps of migrating whales could be seen. Their roiling bodies were accompanied by the sound of expelled breaths as they resurfaced on their journey south from their summer stay in the food-rich waters of the arctic sea. Their presence was somehow comforting to the party, even as the colossal figures were sometimes seen as monsters to the superstitious Norse.

In the distance along their route were cliffs of staggeringly primitive and alluring ice, with yet more snowy precipices stretching into uninhabited fjords that broke off into the interior of the country to their side. Huddled into their boats, the party cringed against the extreme conditions, enduring the discomfort with the heat generated by their own exertions and focusing ahead with single-minded determination.

The small vessels proceeded in a single line, slowly advancing into the never-ending and untamed nature that surrounded them. Erik and Kristian were located in the last of the boats, moving their strokes in careful rhythm as they sought to keep the most efficient pace without burning up all of their energy in the process.

Gazing around, Erik was able to see and gauge the entirety of the party's progress through the gently churning sea. The boat directly in front of them held Sigri and Thorstein, who, along with their heavy gear and servants, were forcing the party to move slower than Erik would have wanted.

As Kristian drove his oar through the water, he stared at the back of Sigri's head, keeping her in focus and not paying attention to much else. At first, this irritated Erik, but over time he realized his son was stuck in a similar circumstance as his own. His first love was but a few meters across the icy sea, but she was forever unattainable and just out of his reach.

This caused a morose sense of loss in Erik's own thoughts, as he understood it was the same with him as for his son; Erik's own dear wife was also just across a cold and forbidding barrier, permanently out of reach of his affections, no matter how much he wished it to be otherwise. Granted, Kristian was in this position for a different reason, but the result of loneliness and loss was precisely the same. Reaching over, Erik patted Kristian on the shoulder, as if to say, *I know your mourning and sense of despair, and all will be well.*

As the waning day stole light from the sky, far to the right, a rocky coastline came into view. Because it was the first stretch of land that had not been encased in ice for some time, it was a welcome sight, and a bit farther ahead, the flat area of a frosty meadow opened up, revealing an open and dry space that was accessible to the shallow drafts of their boats.

In the lead boat, Ketil's voice shouted in recognition of their layover for the night, and he pointed to the shore with an enthusiastic wave of his arms. The entirety of the party recognized their upcoming destination, and on each vessel, their features became happy as they saw their laborious day coming to an end.

All four boats banked toward their destination of Black Meadows, which was neither black nor unwelcome as a place of refuge from the forbidding sea. Night was incoming, but shelter, rest, and food were now at hand.

#

Night had fully arrived on the cold plain, and the sky shone with the light of countless stars. With no other illumination to pollute the experience, the sky was clear and luminescent from the distant pinpricks of their celestial observers. Next to the broad ocean, the open meadow had a commanding view of the space around it, and icebergs and stunted trees were just visible as blurry shadows in the surrounding perimeter.

The hunting party was spread out amongst the shrubs of frozen grass that grew in patches. Three campfires burned in charred, rock-enclosed areas that were obviously used by travelers in the past who required heat and fire for cooking. The vicinity could never be defined as well-traveled, but Norse and Inuit alike had used the meadow to rest and recuperate here for a very long time. Centuries of use were indicated in the soot-filled confines of the ancient stone circles.

Father Galmand sat at the fire that was most close to the ocean and farthest from the surrounding shrubs and struggling trees. His stare locked on the flames as they flickered under a spit with the remains of a rabbit on it. He licked his lips uncontrollably, as if the poor animal was being prepared in the kitchens of one of the finest monarchs of mainland Europe.

Sitting across from Galmand, Erik chuckled at the priest. "Father, it's good to see you appreciate God's creatures. It'll make a fine meal."

Looking embarrassed, Galmand blinked, as if he hadn't noticed Erik at all. He ran his fingers over his simple traveling cloak, suddenly bashful. "I've never been one to shy away from a meal, even that of a recently caught hare."

Erik nodded, letting his grin grow wider. "My mother used to say, 'Only trust a man that enjoys his food.' I think she meant that regarding food, but not so much in drink. I guess that means you're as reliable as they come, priest or not."

Galmand chuckled in response, and his jowls bounced from the movement. "I would be better served if I enjoyed food a little less, but I'm glad your mother would have approved. Obviously, she was a wise lady."

The smile drained somewhat from Erik's face, but he still kept a good mood as he changed the direction of the discussion. "There always seems to be a good supply of seals at Disko, so I hope we'll be having feasts well into the future."

Galmand's smile faded, and he considered Erik's words carefully. "When I first came to Greenland, there was food for all: beef, mutton, goats, and plenty of hay to feed them. No man lived in want of anything. I miss that. Even as a young and inexperienced priest, there was more joy to be had. Families smiled…and there were more of us."

"Yeah, times were better," said Erik, clearly agreeing with the sentiment of better times in the past. "But now, the cold makes our way of life…"

"Much harder," Galmand said, finishing off Erik's words.

Erik mulled over the dialog as the fire crackled on. Sounds of talking and laughs from the other campfires made it seem less lonely in this painfully remote area. Erik considered how it was funny that a little companionship went a long way to increasing a man's optimism, even when nothing else had changed in his outlook.

Such optimism made Erik brave enough to ask a question that was not often spoken aloud. He was tired of avoiding the issue that affected everyone in the settlement to equal degrees. "Do…you think we can continue…like this? With so little around us, and no prospects for a better future?"

Galmand was surprised by the question, but unlike many in the village, he was not offended to face the truth behind the query. His caring expression showed no fear in his answer.

"I think…" replied Galmand, "that life is not meant to be easy. 'Enter through the narrow gate, for the road to destruction is broad, and many choose that route.'"

Erik grinned, but his eyes were serious in the flickering light. "I can always count on you for a biblical quote, and that is certainly true. But…for how long can we pursue this narrow road?"

Galmand rubbed his hands next to the fire. He seemed to have forgotten about the greasy rabbit and his upcoming meal, and he extended his arms towards the area around them, indicating the broad world in the darkness. "Our Inuit friends do well in this environment. Do you see them complaining about the cold, or God's bounty? Maybe it is us that have been on the broad path for too long, without perhaps knowing it?"

Startled, Erik tilted his head, as if he had suddenly been made privy to a truth he should have known all his life. After a moment of silence, he nodded. "I hadn't ever thought of it that way, Father. It…seems your studies in religion made you into a wise man."

Galmand merely grinned in response, and his attention returned to the roasting rabbit.

From the dark, Kristian moved into the circle of light near the fire, sitting next to his father and smiling at Galmand. Unaware of their weighty conversation, he sounded relaxed and in a good mood. "So, who gets the first choice on the meat?"

#

From the campfire farthest from Galmand, Sigri sat and stared into the flames with a sour and scrunched-up face. Looking unhappy seemed to be an emotional state that had grown into an everyday occurrence for her, and she pursed her lips as she considered the fate of the village and her place in it.

Stealing a glance over to Kristian's campfire, she frowned further. It would seem her former love had suddenly adapted well to his surroundings, and for some reason, that seemed to bother her. She had no designs on the young man, life had offered her a way to improve everything for herself and her family, but something about her former relationship seemed unsettled. She yearned for finality, a point of mutual acceptance between Kristian and herself about their new stations in life, but it seemed that was never to happen. This made her irritated, she realized, but she couldn't quite understand why.

Returning her gaze to the flames, she sighed and fell back into considerations of how much food would be retrieved from this hunting venture. She hoped it was enough for all the people she had known and called friends all these years of her young life.

Thorstein entered the fire's light from the side and sat down next to her. Showing a smile to Sigri, he tried to appear upbeat. "This is going well. It's not such a bad place to visit."

Sigri looked at him and nodded, giving him a slight smile. Just then, one of their servants brought two trays of food, which she and Thorstein accepted with a polite nod. The food was an extravagant dish of potatoes and cooked fowl, a luxury for the best of times in Greenland. For a journey into the deep arctic, it was positively foolish.

As Thorstein began to eat, Sigri responded to his observation. "This is such a beautiful area—untouched and unchanged since God created it. Few people have ever walked this meadow, and I think few ever will."

Scanning the darkness around them, Thorstein replied with a concerned nod, like he was worried about what else may have walked this area. Still, he put on a brave face. "Indeed, it is. I can see its attraction to you and your people."

Sigri scowled at this but remained silent. She realized that for all his talk of being one people that colonized this area from Iceland, he was quick to categorize these people as her people. After a bit of self-reflection, though, she understood that he was just following her own lead in making his background and people so different than hers.

Breathing deep, she contemplated relationships and cultures, even ones that should be so similar. Truth was, they were never easy, wherever you came from, and with whomever you tried to have a relationship with.

From the side, Rand walked in. Plate in hand, he licked his fingers and sat across from Sigri and Thorstein. Noticeably, he avoided meeting Thorstein's eyes as he spoke between bites of his meal.

"This is what the Eastern Settlement looked like before our ancestors tamed it," Rand said, peering at his daughter—but not her husband. "It's what men of decision do, make a future for their people, without separating them."

Thorstein took in the insult, noticing the latent hostility from Rand with a frown. Unfortunately, or perhaps fortunately for family peace, he was too preoccupied with scanning the darkness around them to formulate a response.

From a rocky outcropping only a hundred yards away, the dark eyes of the Keelut returned Thorstein's look. The rich merchant could not have known the creature was there, but the Keelut's focus was clear in the night.

Crouched down to avoid detection and aided by nearly perfect vision in the darkness, the Keelut focused on the group, moving its gaze between Thorstein, Rand, and Sigri. Afterward, it scanned the other campfires, taking in the other hunters across the clearing as they went about eating.

In time, its eyes came to rest on Erik and Kristian, then Galmand. Stopping there, the Keelut's hostile gaze examined the priest with intense and unerring attention, as if nothing else in the camp mattered.

#

Entwined in his cloak and furry animal skins, Erik slumbered on the floor of the tent. Snoring gently, he looked like a peaceful cat that had reached its maximum state of relaxation and contentedness. To his side sprawled Kristian, who had one leg draped half-over his father as they dozed together in the cramped interior of their cozy sleeping spot.

Vague light from the stars and moon seeped in from the open flap of the flimsy tent. The night and camp outside were utterly quiet and still, and even the sound of the constant wind was reduced to a gentle whoosh.

A loud roar broke the night's silence, followed by terrified screams and wails of frightened men. The intensity of the sounds was shocking, forcing Erik and Kristian awake with a suddenness that left them reeling in exhausted confusion.

Stumbling up, they each grabbed their weapons, taking time to look at each other with startled eyes in the tent's shadows. Pushing outside, they scanned around, trying to understand what was happening.

The field around them was enveloped in a dense and frightful fog that seemed to cloy at everything, adding to the confusion of their sleep-addled brains. Visibility was only a few yards into the night, with everything hazy and obscured by the rampant mist.

More screams broke through the fog, and Kristian and Erik held their unsheathed weapons defensively, horrified as they searched for an unknown attacker. Squinting to see something, anything, they stepped slowly forward.

A polar bear leapt into view from the roiling mist, fierce and huge against the backdrop of fading campfires. It reared up and bellowed a bizarre, blood-curdling wail, like it was a beast from a wicked nightmare. Its eyes appeared black and lifeless, and when it snarled and turned its head with a looping ferocity, it was like a terrible demon to the shocked onlookers.

In the bear's back was stuck a long spear, buried to a depth of six inches. Black blood seeped from the wound, but it seemed unaffected as it spun in circles, lashing out with its enormous claws at the two men who had been on guard and now struggled to fend it off. The tormented animal's wails were fierce…and otherworldly, like its primitive brain was bathed in some unknown and intense agony.

Emerging from tents and stepping from the fog were other members of the party. With stunned expressions and confused shouts, the companions rushed forward, clutching various poled weapons in their hands. The men surged on the offensive, poking at the animal with the savage and practiced thrusts of people accustomed to such dangers and well-practiced in the art of combat.

But the bear was unaffected by the attacks, even as two more spears were plunged deep into its belly. The beast's blood was everywhere, and it continually spun, looking for a victim amongst the attacking and feinting hunters.

With a great swipe of its black-clawed paw, the animal lunged forward, and two men were smacked backward with a jarring crunch on the rocky ground. The animal appeared invulnerable, whatever the damage inflicted on it.

Focusing ahead, Erik abruptly rushed forward and leapt toward the bear's back as it wheeled toward Sigmar. Extending his arms up, Erik rammed his longsword down, piercing it deep between its ribs and burying the blade to the hilt. Helplessly skewered, the crazed animal moaned a sorrowful whimper and collapsed.

Rushing to his father's side, Kristian joined Erik in his attack, and after the animal slumped to the ground, Kristian stuck his long knife into the hide of the bear, slicing into its neck, its armpit, its back—anywhere he could to ensure its immediate death. Over several moments, father and son struck yet more mortal blows into the fallen beast, ramming their weapons again and again into its tough flesh.

Their companions rushed forward to help, but seeing nothing else to be done, they merely watched the thrusts continue. The bear's black and viscous blood was flung about the area in spurts, and Erik and Kristian were covered in it as they repeatedly pierced the carcass with manic thrusts of their sharp blades.

After a while, the mist seemed to pull back, and the meadow's open nature was again revealed as the fog rolled away and disappeared. Erik and Kristian stopped their attacks and looked up from their grisly work, breathing in great gasps as they stared at the other participants of the fight.

All was once again silent, and the expressions of the party members were fearful and expectant as they scanned the surrounding darkness for any other threats.

From far across the inland side of the meadow, the Keelut watched the hunters. Tilting its hellish head, it continued staring, as if bewildered by the outcome of the fight. It focused for some time, fixing its soulless eyes entirely on Erik and Kristian.

Turning around, its now-camouflaged form slunk away from the meadow and was lost in the dark and frozen interior of the barren island.

# Chapter Eleven

Morning mist drifted through the isolated meadow, obscuring the primitive view of icy mountains in the distant interior of Greenland. As clinging fog rolled across the plant-starved field, the shapes of the hunting companions were intermittently shrouded by the mist, looking as if they were ghostly images repetitively carrying out some eternal duty in the growing light of day.

Pinging from simple tools rang through the morning air as several of the party members disassembled their basic tent structures from the night's camp, while others carried supplies to be loaded on ships for the next phase of their journey north.

Ketil and Sigmar carried an injured man between them on a makeshift stretcher toward the shoreline. Stepping gingerly next to the party's beached boats, they carefully set the man on the ground next to another wounded companion from the night's harrowing battle with the crazed bear. Walking away, their temperaments were sour and depressed as they paced toward the crumpled outline of the slain bear in the middle of the nearly packed-up camp.

Simple bloodied bandages covered the head and face of one man, while the other was bound tightly in skins against the cold. The second man's face was nearly covered under the fluffy animal hair of his blankets, but what could be seen of his sallow complexion showed the worrying pallor of a man with potential internal injuries.

Galmand and Sigri attended to both men, keeping them comfortable in the freezing breeze that had picked up across the sea's rolling waves. Neither looked happy about their survival prospects—or what saving them might mean for their mission to retrieve food for the village.

Galmand made the sign of the cross over each of the men, then stepped back with a worried frown. Behind him, Erik, Kristian, Thorstein, and Rand flashed similar concerns as they stared down at the injured.

"Will they…be alright?" asked Kristian.

Moving his gaze up to the cloud-streaked sky, Erik shook his head and breathed in the brisk air. Keeping his voice low, his tone was not optimistic. "I don't know. The injuries are severe…I never saw a white bear attack like that. It was like it was out of its mind, even for a beast."

Stepping closer to the other men, Galmand showed a tired smile and gestured back to the wounded men. "They may survive, God willing, but they must return to the Eastern Settlement. They are in no condition to go with us on the hunt."

Erik walked forward and bent over one of the men, moving a blanket to make sure he was comfortable. Standing fully erect, Erik stretched his back and motioned south, toward where they had come from the day before. "I'll take 'em back. The rest of you need to continue up to Disko. The risks are too high to wait. You oughta be able to fit enough dead seals onto three boats to make it work."

It was quiet for a time as everyone considered the best course for the group. Shaking his head, Rand was the first to respond.

"Not a good idea," Rand said, and he chewed on his lip as looked toward one of the boats. "You'll be needed here. It is you that's best suited for this type of work."

"That is a horrific idea, I think," interjected Thorstein, surprising the party with his own loud tone, one that was full of conviction and some reluctance. "You are the best with the harpoon, I am told."

Erik scowled and looked among the men present, then over to the others who were preparing for departure.

"Who, then?" asked Erik, facing Thorstein and clearly unhappy with their unfolding choices. "You? You couldn't row your way up a small creek."

Smiling but not offended, Thorstein thought for a moment. Gesturing to his servants, his cold gaze fell on Erik. "Ditmar and

Elias can operate a boat as well as anyone. When we get back, I will ensure the injured are well cared for—I'll put them up in my own home if need be. No expense will be spared. The rest of you can continue as before."

Worried, Sigri stepped away from her overwatch of the wounded men. Placing her hand gently on Thorstein's back, her concern was palpable at this proposed course of action, though she remained quiet.

Rand nodded, giving an impressed look to Thorstein for the first time in a long while. Pointing to his daughter, his tone was respectful but determined. "That makes sense, but she is staying with me. She's as good as me on the hunt, and I won't let her out of my sight until we get back. If she goes back, I am going with her."

Alarmed, Thorstein's eyes bulged while he contemplated being away from his wife in such a potentially dangerous circumstance. He gazed over at Kristian accusingly, like the young man might well have planned this series of events. For his part, Kristian avoided his interrogating glare, finding more interesting things to look at on the empty ocean to the side of the camp.

Stepping forward, Rand patted Thorstein on the shoulder, letting his voice sound pleasant and accommodating. "She will be safe with me, Thorstein. On my honor. She will be taken care of…and watched over."

Except for Kristian, Thorstein moved his stare amongst the accompanying group of people on this cold and distant meadow next to the frigid sea so far from home. As their eyes met his, each of the party members looked back with some measure of hope and a new respect for the merchant, like they were seeing him in a new light—and maybe he was more than the figure they had come to know and perhaps disliked.

These Greenlanders had all watched Thorstein cut a path of privilege through their close-knit community, always doing what was best for him and his business interests, even as he was the last of the traders willing to brave the icy seas from Iceland to get to their outpost of civilization at the end of the world. To a man, none expected Thorstein to leave his wife in the care of others to save men who had no importance or bearing on his own life.

Thorstein could picture in their eyes the potential disdain they would have for his ego and selfishness as they awaited his reply. Moments passed in quiet anticipation. Sigri moved closer to him, leaning in to offer him support due to the anguished decision he had to make.

Breathing deep, Thorstein nodded his acceptance of the plan for him to return with the wounded. He even managed a meek smile as he got himself mentally prepared to serve others for the first time he could ever remember.

#

Thorstein's two servants struggled while carrying the last heavy bags of goods that had been brought on the expedition.

Breathing hard and swaying from the effort, they grunted and hefted the supplies over the ridge of one of the boats beached along the frozen earth of the rocky shoreline.

Gently swaying in the surf, the craft was perched on dark volcanic soil under foamy waves splashing against the shore. Hauling themselves up, the fatigued attendants dragged themselves over the edge of the vessel and prepared the boat for departure by setting their supplies alongside the injured hunters lying on the boat's wooden bottom. Below them, both wounded men dozed under the murky light of the day's overcast sky.

After arranging themselves and stretching their muscles, the harried servants looked up expectantly. They each held an oar and looked excited to be returning to the village, away from the bizarre violence of the night before, and they even managed a faint smile at Thorstein as they got into position to row for an extended period.

Standing some distance from his waiting boat, Thorstein nodded approvingly at his men. Turning his attention to his wife, he locked Sigri in a firm hug and frowned due to his imminent departure. "I will get these men back…and wait for you. Please stay close to your father."

Sigri noticed Thorstein's unease at the predicament of leaving her to continue without him. Nodding, she leaned into his chest with a genuine smile. "I will be true to you, whatever the cost. I am not perfect, but I keep my word when I give it—especially in important matters. But you must make certain you keep yours and…wait for us."

Nodding grimly but happy with her reply, Thorstein moved his gaze up from Sigri and stared over the vast ocean he was soon to travel. It was a raw and untamed sea, with forbidding icebergs and freezing water that meant certain death for any traveler with the misfortune to fall into it.

Thorstein was an experienced sailor who could make his way easily on one of his many cargo ships, but he was unused to travel in such a constricting environment. The wrong navigational move or misread of the currents would end in a mortal trip to the bottom of the ocean or slow death by starvation from being stranded in a shipwreck.

The reason Thorstein had first found his way to this enormous island of Greenland was because it was no longer visited by other traders. The original route of travel centuries earlier had been to move directly west from Iceland, run into this vast piece of land, then sail south around the tip of Greenland to find the way to these settlements. Over time that route had become clogged with dangerous ice, forcing mariners to abandon the prior course and instead, set out across open water to reach these shores.

Such a direction was safer from icebergs but also made the dangers of the open ocean and its currents more pronounced. It was simply too big a risk for other captains to make at the present. Over time, the best way of making the voyage had been forgotten, and many ships had been lost at sea while trying to navigate it.

Thorstein knew that with risk came reward, so he worked out a particular route that was not widely known to other ships, and that direction had paid him and his family handsomely over time. The prices for the hides, rope, falcons, and tusks from Greenland were originally robust, but had dropped in concert with the colder weather that always seemed to move farther south with each year in this new century.

Even the horn of a particular seal that inhabited these waters, which Thorstein had long been able to pass off as that of a unicorn, had come under increasing skepticism in the European continent under the new thinking of the church and several universities, which wanted proof of the existence of the mythical horse. Under pressure to provide a substantiating unicorn carcass, Thorstein had quietly dropped the horns from his common packing lists and said there seemed to be no more of the beasts to harvest.

Now, what was available to buy and sell in common trade was no longer profitable. His prospects had dried up entirely, making his continued presence here senseless and without a workable way to move forward.

With Sigri, Thorstein had hoped to build a family and future from his commercial ventures, but the reality was that their plans would have to be with other forms of trade in new areas of the wider world. Whether moving to capitalize on the growing fisheries of cod in the North Atlantic or seeking to leverage their location in Iceland to trade with the newly ascendant English and their larger ships, everything he had done up to this point was going to have to change.

Thorstein was perhaps not totally honest about his intentions to abandon Greenland to its fate, but in the end, Sigri would have to see that it was the only logical thing he could do. A good businessman knew his limits and learned to adapt to reality, however unsettling or cruel it was. Her father would escape with her to Thorstein's estates and live a pampered life, but the rest of the population was going to have to make their own lives in the reality of the new colder climate. He had just enough ships to extract his goods from this area and flee, but there was no additional room for Sigri's people, even assuming they wanted to leave.

Letting his thoughts return to the present, Thorstein smiled down at his pretty wife and kissed her a final time before slowly walking to the waiting boat. After climbing in, he was pushed out into the dark water by several of the hunters, and as his men worked their oars to head south, he and Sigri shared a longing stare. Their features were calm at their parting of ways, but distress and worry hid just under their expressions while his boat became smaller in the distance.

From farther in the camp, another group member watched Thorstein leave. Kristian was contemplative as he watched the small vessel disappear on its way south from the camp's position, and he stared after it even after it was swallowed by the forever mists that made extended visibility so difficult on the sea.

Looking to the back of Sigri's head, Kristian continued his pondering stare, focusing his thoughts and energy on his former love. He wondered with almost a detached sense of intrigue what could be going through her thoughts now, or even if she still managed to think of him at all in her busy mind. She had always been the smart one between them, always planning for the next best thing, and just now Kristian realized the next best thing decidedly did not include him—he was never to be part of her future schemes.

After some time, Sigri must have felt his attention, and she moved her eyes defensively back his way. She was not hostile to meet his gaze, but neither was her appraisal of him warm or inviting. For several torturous moments, they peered at each other, as if they were uncertain combatants that would someday need to thrash out their differences on the field of battle. That upcoming conflict would not be physical combat, be it would be necessary just the same.

Erik walked up to Kristian's side, momentarily breaking the contest of wills. As Kristian glanced at his father, Sigri took the opportunity to move away from her vantage point, and she paced toward the place where Rand had already prepared their things for the next stage of their trip.

Erik met his son's eyes with a stern and implacable grimace, and although he didn't reproach his son, there was warning enough in his expression to prevent Kristian from further exploring the brief moment he shared with Sigri. Embarrassed and uncomfortable, Kristian gazed down at the ground.

Striding up, Ketil interrupted, peering at Erik with a surprised, almost crazed look. "Ye aren't gonna believer it, Erik. The bear's meat is bad."

Erik faced Ketil, nodding with an understanding grin. "I'm not fond of the taste, either. But we can't let it go to waste. Every bit of food we take—."

"Not that," responded Ketil, and he pointed back to the crumpled and sliced remains of the huge bear. "It's really bad, like it's been spoiled in the sun. Ye all get sick if ye eat it."

Erik stood with his face tilted, like he didn't or couldn't know what Ketil meant. He seemed unable to process what could have caused it to turn bad so quickly.

Taking the chance to involve his own thoughts in something other than Sigri, Kristian cleared his throat. Stepping between them, Kristian gazed at Ketil, trying to figure out what he meant.

"How is that possible?" asked Kristian, looking perplexed. "No meat spoils like that anywhere. Especially in the freezing cold."

Ketil shook his head in response, clearly unsure of the answer.

Looking back at his father, Kristian also saw that his father was confused and unsure. In silence, all three men retained their bewilderment as their companions throughout the camp completed their preparations for the continued journey to Disko Bay.

#

Erik smiled as he squinted into the afternoon sun. To his side, Galmand matched his grin, and farther in the back of the boat, Kristian was also smiling as he paddled ahead. To Kristian's side was another young and excited-looking villager, Gabriel, who sloshed his own oar through the water in synchronized harmony as they pushed the craft across a placid spread of ocean.

Their boat glided across a beautiful stretch of pristine and calm water, with numerous mini-icebergs dotting the rippling surface far into the distance. The sun shone at an angle, indicating the end of summer was fast approaching, but its welcome rays painted the water's surface in such a way as to make the area momentarily bright and pleasant, despite the numbing temperature. For the moment, it appeared the expedition was on some grand and comfortable outing amongst the primitive and captivating scenery.

Ahead of Erik's boat, the other two craft were also making headway towards a series of higher and stouter icebergs, ones that held whole colonies of seals sunning themselves. Not concerned with the incoming Norse hunters, the seals slipped in and out of the water as they jostled for space on their freezing and slick mass, appearing like milling ants on the top of their icy islands.

Reaching down, Erik's grin grew wider still, and he patted the rough carcass of a dead seal with a wet thump of his hand against its waterproof skin. "At this rate, we can get what we need in one day. They're practically begging us to fill our cargo."

Nodding, Galmand was in a similar mindset, and he scanned the horizon ahead with a deep and appreciative expression, showing his thankfulness for the bounty bestowed on their brief trip to sea. After a moment's thought, however, some worry crept into his features as other considerations crossed his mind.

"I only hope the Western Settlement greets us on time," Galmand said. "They have undoubtedly caught their fill for the winter, so they should greet us with a mountain more of meat. With luck, they will allow us to carry the excess in one of their small boats home, allowing us to make it past the winter more easily."

Erik grinned at the hope of even more food for the upcoming cold season. They had struggled through the prior Winter with barely a month's rations to spare, so the inclination to expect more from their present hunt made him momentarily optimistic.

"Ungertok has always been on time," said Erik, referring to the leader of the Western Settlement. "They have always lived close to the Inuit and relied on their food sources more, while we've tried to keep to the old ways of pastures and livestock. Now, I think he chose the right approach, and I'll be happy to tell him that when we meet."

Fifty yards to the side opposite of the expansive seascape, the shore was flat and spread out far to either side—ahead and behind them. Empty of vegetation except for some scattered brush, the coastal plain of this far northern area continued inward for several miles. In the distance, the flat ground climbed to frost-colored hills, then farther to precipitous mountains locked in ice shelves and eternal glaciers.

The three boats glided silently on, their paddles working diligently towards the approaching colony of seals. In the lead vessel, Sigri was also in good humor, and her eyes positively glowed as she exchanged a victorious grin with her father. At her feet in the hold, she had her own dead seal, and its blood colored a small pool of water in the bottom of the craft. Next to the animal lay her wicked-looking harpoon, its end covered in gore from its recent use.

To the outside of Sigri and Rand sat Annar and Niels, who rowed in coordinated swishes towards their goal. They were older—Niels was even into middle age—and neither looked optimistic as they hardened themselves for an extended period of effort in this all-important chase for seal flesh.

From the middle boat, Sigmar inclined his head to the side, noticing something. He called out in a commanding voice, his worried tone disturbing the silent and mellow environment. "Aye, Erik, look to the port."

From the left of their path, a bank of fog rolled toward the boats, seemingly emerging out of nowhere. The fog appeared…bizarre, churning with a milky and glowing sheen as it seemed to aim for the vessels. It was not something seen on the sea by any of the hunters before, and all three vessels focused into the mass with distressed and unsure gazes.

Erik grew immediately concerned, and he panned his head to take in the full extent of the oncoming wall of mist. Thinking quickly, he reached down and grabbed a coil of thick rope. Holding it up for the other boats to see, he shouted in alarm. "Tie up. We need to stay together."

As the odd bank of clouds moved toward the small flotilla, the companions quickly passed ropes between each other and cinched themselves together. With the task completed, they waited to be enveloped by the dense fog.

As the mist passed over them, visibility dropped to a precious few feet. Barely able to see each other in their own boats, they became like small islands, with only a bit of coiled line to make them feel part of the wider effort. They passed there for several minutes, gently calling out to each other across the short lengths, as if making too much noise was something to be avoided in the stifling fog. Their boats bobbed there in the tendrilled fog, and a sense of foreboding spread amongst the companions, tickling at their dark perceptions of impending danger in this remote and chilly area.

On Erik's boat, the water lapped against the wooden hull in mild waves. Erik and Galmand traded worried gazes, not knowing what to do in the confined and blinded space. To the back, Kristian and Gabriel looked outwards, holding up their oars in a base expression of some kind of primeval need for self-protection.

"Aiyee," came the shout from another of the boats. A large splash followed the sound, followed by panicked screams from other areas in unseen depths of the surrounding mist.

The confused party's eyes shot about, searching for the source of the panic. Kristian held his oar above his head, ready to strike out as yet more struggles and shouts came from ahead, while Gabriel unintentionally moved closer to the direct middle of the boat with scared eyes.

Trying to gauge what was happening, Erik was confused and terrified as he pivoted in the uneven boat. Licking his lips, he placed his hand on his sword, trying to keep his balance in the floundering craft. Looking back to Kristian, he pointed toward the direction of the shore and shouted. "Row for the shore. Everyone make it to land."

Gabriel and Kristian moved to comply, but their vessel was quickly stopped by the rope running taut towards the next boat in the fog. They were stuck in place.

From farther out, Rand's voice broke through the chaos around them. "Sigri, swim for it. I'm behind you." Two splashes into the freezing water followed his words.

Drawing a simple fishing knife, Kristian began sawing through the attached line, trying to cut free. When it was cut, he and Gabriel sloshed their paddles into the water, and the boat started moving toward their perceived goal of safety on dry land.

From the water, the Keelut sprang with frightening speed, landing with some grace near Gabriel. With shocking speed, it batted Gabriel aside, and he twisted and plunged overboard with a grunt. Looking back toward Kristian, the creature was immediately swatted across the face with the crunch of Kristian's forcefully swung paddle. The force of the blow was sufficient to shatter the oar into splinters.

Seemingly unhurt, the Keelut shook off the attack and advanced toward the back of the craft, holding up a bloody claw from the end of its sickly white arm, as if it wanted to gut Kristian with a simple slash of its razor-like nails. Kristian tried to escape, falling backward as he reached to his waist for his long knife. Unable to extract the weapon in time, he held up his arms in a fruitless attempt to save himself.

A thwicking sound came from the front of the boat, and a crossbow bolt buried into the back neck of the fetid Keelut. Spinning about, the surprised creature stared over to see Erik crouching over his crossbow, trying to reload the ungainly weapon.

Focusing ahead to measure its new enemy, the beast was unaffected by the sharp missile, and it didn't move to extract the barbed quarrel, even as its bloody and sharp end protruded from the front of its neckline. Instead, its black eyes immediately found Galmand crouching in fear to the side. Stepping over the dead seal, the Keelut advanced toward the cowering priest, unbothered by the uneven pitch of the craft and ignoring Erik.

From behind, Kristian slammed the broken end of the oar into the back of the beast, knocking it forward. Several shards of the wooden end pierced deep into its otherworldly skin, but with a surging spin, the Keelut turned and swatted Kristian from the boat. The power of the blow lifted him from the floor and flung him into the mist, followed by a lonely splash into the sea.

Moving with freakish speed, the monster was almost a blur as it grabbed Galmand's ankle. Yanking the overweight priest with some ease, it tried to drag him overboard and was only stopped by Galmand grabbing a support brace on the floor to avoid being pulled into the water. The clergyman wailed in horrid fear as he clung to a metal-hinged wooden piece, praying with his bulging eyes and terrified screams to avoid being pulled away. His body was lifted from the ground as the fiendishly strong Keelut repeatedly tried to tug him free from his handhold.

With a wet thump, Erik brought the blade of his family's old sword down, severing the Keelut's arm above the wrist. Its soulless eyes going wide, the creature held up its stumped limb, and black liquid pumped wildly from it.

An inhuman and frightful wail emerged from its hideous fanged mouth as the creature focused on Erik and his sword. Blood from the Keelut coated the surface of the weapon, and a hissing sound came from the boiling fluid as it sizzled against the ancient metal blade.

Leaping into the mist, the Keelut fled. Only the continued shouts and splashes around them were left as witnesses to its assault. Rushing to the edge of the boat, Erik leaned over and searched for his son in the murky water. Seeing Kristian struggling to stay afloat, he reached his panicked hand down to him.

"Give me your hand," shouted Erik, and as Kristian grabbed onto his fingers, Erik raised his voice above the mayhem that surrounded them. "Everyone hold on. Let me know where you're at. I'll come to you."

Muffled cries from the fog answered Erik, and as suddenly as it had come, the mist began to dissipate, flowing back over the waves as it withdrew from the area.

Erik was glad to see the fog disappear but just then noticed sea water was filling the bottom of their suddenly leaky boat. As Galmand shakily rose to help pull Kristian aboard, their worried eyes moved from the inflowing water to focus on the deserted shoreline. They had to hurry or there would be no rescuers left.

# Chapter Twelve

The Norse boat lay partially out of the water on the desolate shoreline. It had two ragged holes in its bottom, as if the wooden hull had been punctured with the directed force of some small and dense object.

On the rocky shore near it stood Erik, Niels, Kristian, Galmand, Sigri, Rand, Ketil, and Sigmar. The group of hunters stared down with disbelieving and disturbed eyes, processing the scene with the exasperated gazes of people who have seen something and can't yet come to terms with it.

Below them, Gabriel lay face up on the rocky earth, sprawled with his back arched and head craned to the side, as if he didn't wish to see what was above him. His arms were held up and curled back, like he had tried to ward something off in a failed attempt at self-protection.

His eyes were missing from his sockets, having been torn brutally from his surprised death-mask face. The red gristle of interior skull tissue and brain matter protruded from the open holes, leaving the young man without the benefit of a peaceful death pose to be remembered by.

Looking away from Gabriel, Erik wiped away tears of shock and mourning. His voice was low and evidenced a sense of horrified worry. "I couldn't find the other two. With the cold water, it's already too late…"

As Erik's voice trailed off, he also grieved for the loss of Annar from Sigri's boat, as well as Valtur, a quiet gray-haired man who had been with Ketil's group. They had both dove into the water to escape the Keelut during the attack, but no evidence of their fate was now evident in the ocean or on the shoreline.

The numbers of the companions had shrunk dramatically, and the loss would be felt in a direct and striking way in the village. Death was an unfortunate aspect of life on a frontier that often called for risky endeavors to be taken in support of providing for the community, but as the Norse population dwindled, each loss was felt in an increasingly outsized manner. The lack of sufficient working people was not a shortfall that could easily be remedied.

Erik and Galmand had managed to stay mostly dry during the heinous assault by the creature, but the other party members shivered under cloaks and skins as they stood in silence. Focusing down on Gabriel and then out over the forbidding sea, the place where two of their boats now lay at the bottom, the face of each companion was withdrawn and fearful.

Every person who had just been killed was known and cared for by all, with no anonymity from personal knowledge to hide the pain of loss. Tragedy was always amplified by personal relationships, and in this, all the survivors shared personal bonds with the deceased, making their deaths a crushing loss. Where only a few hundred people shared a common life in the settlement, every neighbor was well-known and often relied upon to help deal with the struggles of life.

Breathing deep, Erik paced over to the beached vessel. Reaching inside, he plucked the Keelut's black-clawed white hand from the boat's interior. Striding back, he held out the pale, otherworldly limb for all to see. Its almost translucent skin was covered in an oily sheen, like the Keelut had excreted the thick liquid straight from its abominable pores. The foul appendage shimmered weirdly in the light as Erik turned it over to examine the strange body part.

"What demon could…?" asked Galmand, pointing at the hand, his voice quiet and disbelieving.

"It is precisely as the boy said," replied Rand, referring to the surviving boy that had been saved from the farm. "The…devil, and he hunts us even out here. Even in the cold ocean."

Galmand shook his head in response, maintaining his incredulous stare. "Why…how?"

It wasn't lost on the rest of the party that the priest, supposedly the one with the most faith in God, was taking the existence of a devilish creature among them in a more difficult manner. While the others took the situation for what it was,

Galmand appeared more broadly affected by the repercussions of a devil apparently sent from the other side of God's supernatural ledger.

"Father," said Sigri, speaking softly between shivers. "There's evil in the world. Usually, it's the kind we're used to, but this is…something else."

It became quiet, and Galmand looked back out to sea, his eyes fearful and overwhelmed.

Kristian cleared his throat, biting back the trauma he felt from nearly dying just a few minutes before. He moved his hand over the large swollen mark across his cheek where he had been struck by the Keelut. "It moved like nothing I've ever seen. Strong as…anything."

Looking back from the sea, Galmand nodded. Having collected himself, his demeanor grew calmer as he talked. "It was after me, like Father Sturlesson and the Inuit shamans."

Looking over to Erik, Galmand touched his throat in a protective manner as he considered the recent attack. Shaking his head, he puzzled over what exactly transpired. "You shot it with your crossbow, but nothing happened. Nothing living could take such a wound without worry. But…when you struck it with your sword…"

The rest of the party looked at Erik, their eyes growing quizzical as they focused on his weapon. Responding to their unspoken query, Erik unsheathed the sword and held it up. The sun's rays shone off the pale metal, and no blood was now visible on its clean surface.

Holding his blade in one hand and the Keelut's limb in the other, Erik's expression was a combination of bafflement and trepidation, like he didn't know what to say or how to proceed. He traded glances with the rest of the party as everyone considered what any of it meant.

Stepping close, Galmand peered closely at Erik's sword. In the pommel of the weapon was a metal insignia of a cross. It was faded, but the cross was distinct and colored red over a dark black shield. "What is this?"

Erik held it closer to Galmand, allowing a thorough inspection. "It's been in my family for generations. Brought it here from Norway, but never had a need for it."

Tilting his head, Rand also stepped in to get a better look at the sword. He motioned to Erik for permission to examine it, and Erik handed it to him pommel-first.

Holding it close to his aged eyes and squinting, Rand searched his memory for some distant recollection. Nodding, he spoke softly. "I have seen this cross before as a drawing in an old book in my library. I think it is from some order of knights set up hundreds of years ago. I…think they were in the Holy Land…but they came from somewhere else before that. I don't recall the name, but that was certainly their crest."

Stepping next to his father, Kristian drew his own knife and held it next to the longer sword. Both had the same insignia in the hilt, like they were a matched pair.

Sigri spoke louder now, pointing to both weapons. "Why would your ancestors have blades from the Holy Land? Don't they make their own in Norway? From the books I've read about the Vikings, our blades were prized throughout the world. Why would they need these?"

Staying quiet, Erik appeared unsure and uneasy. "The blades weren't from the Holy Land; they only went there later with knights who embarked on the Crusades. Long before that, Norway was converted by the Church. It was said that before this conversion the people there were wicked, and evil was often found among them. Maybe these swords were brought at that time?"

Kristian nodded, sounding scared—but also undaunted. "And…I can't be the only one here to notice that Norway is also a place where icebergs and mountains of snow are, right? Maybe Greenland isn't the first place this devil has been found? Maybe we're not the first to face them."

Taking the sword back from Rand, Erik showed his son an approving look as he thought over his idea. As was often the case, it was not unusual in any line of work or discussion that the least experienced person could come up with the best questions or answers involving a problem.

Sighing, Erik also considered the puzzle of how the recent fight had ended. Dropping the Keelut's hand on the ground, he pressed it under his leather boot, then set the point of the sharp blade on the white flesh, as if wanting to run it through again for good measure.

"Maybe they also knew more about this devil than we do," Erik said, and he glanced at each of the party members, finally nodding with some satisfaction. "If that's true, we can thank them because now, we can defend ourselves."

#

At night, an enormous campfire illuminated the field, casting shifting light over the dispirited camp of hunters. The crackling flames were fueled by piles of scrub brush collected from the area's limited vegetation, as well as from felling two scrawny trees that grew near the end of the barren meadow.

From the darkened ocean, the methodical thrumming of waves against shadowy outcroppings of rock disturbed the air, while grainy light from distant stars ensured all approaches to the encampment could be monitored for any approach by a predator.

A makeshift drying rack comprised of limbs from the diminutive trees stood near the fire, and all manner of woolen clothes dried under its bountiful heat. On one side of the rack sat Erik, Kristian, Rand, and Sigri, while on the other, Galmand and Sigmar dozed under blankets next to the flames' warmth.

Standing farther away to either side, Niels and Ketil faced outward and stood guard, taking their turn to make sure their monstrous tormentor could not sneak up on the group. Notably, the party had adopted Erik's family weapons in shifts, and his longsword and long knife hung from the guards' belts as they protectively scanned the surroundings of the camp.

Taking note of the calm exterior of the area, Rand cocked his head doubtfully at Erik. "Are you sure that is wise? I would think the ocean would be a safer route of retreat."

Erik pressed his lips together, losing patience as he motioned to the dark water at their side. "Were you watching what just happened? That devil swam like a fish and jumped like a dolphin. At least on land, we have a chance."

In response to Rand's continuing skeptical look, Erik huffed and indicated the boat with a motion of his head. "Besides, I'm not even sure we can fix it, even if we wanted to row back home."

Leaning toward Erik, Sigri nodded in apparent agreement, but she sounded as uncertain as her father when she finally spoke. "So, we are to go overland to the Western Settlement? That will take at least three days, and I'm told it can be dangerous by itself, even taking into account the presence of that thing. Anyway, weren't the others from that village supposed to meet us here this evening?"

Breathing deep, Erik showed a concerned look, one that always accompanied a sour mood when he was unsure of an outcome. Unfortunately, the outcome in this case was a far worse and more important matter than he had ever experienced or hoped to address. "They were, and in the fifteen years since

I've been doing this hunt, they were always here early and already camped when we arrived. Maybe they already harvested their fill and moved back to their village? Maybe they got more food from their settlement than us? They could be in better shape than we are."

Rand shook his head, speaking in an unconvinced tone to Erik's wishful thinking. "That's ridiculous. If we assume they are at their village, we can also assume they have less of everything at their homes, except for the seals. The weather up here is even colder, meaning less hay and even fewer domestic animals for meat and milk. In any case, when they haven't kept their word to meet us here, it's a cause for worry. The messenger boat we sent to inquire after finding Father Sturlesson must have told them of a dangerous enemy lurking around."

Erik took a moment before nodding at Rand's logic. It didn't take a learned man to figure out that their world was growing more precarious with each passing day. Silence passed between them as they pondered the next best move to make.

"Maybe we can be honest here?" Kristian asked, adding his voice to the discussion for the first time. "Seems like now would be a good time for it."

Surprised, Rand, Sigri, and even Erik stopped and looked at the bashful young man, who up until now had seemed to follow only Erik's lead in such matters of planning.

"We got exactly one seal to feed us—and no boat to get us home," said Kristian. "Now, we got to get to the other

Settlement and borrow their boats to hunt more meat for the winter. If we don't, our people are going to starve."

After a moment's hesitation, Kristian's cool gaze fell on Sigri. He offered her an annoyed glance before continuing. "Unless we happen to be wealthy."

A look of surprise crossed Sigri's features, and she raised her voice defensively. "Wealth has nothing to do with anything here. We are all in this together, just like always. Why would you say such a thing? You're just—."

Rand cut off his daughter with a raised hand and a look of warning. "There's no need to quarrel here. It's bad enough to deal with that thing out there…hunting us."

Standing, Rand moved to the fire, where he rubbed his hands vigorously near the flames to warm them. For once, his tone moved from confrontation to that of a peacemaker, and he nodded amicably to the other three.

Staring inland, Rand's eyes found the outlines of the trail that would take them to the Western Settlement. Nodding, he knew that barely marked passage by land would be their only path to survival. "My biggest worry is this: what happens if we get to the other village and it's empty? What do we do then?"

#

The pulsing campfire continued to burn bright, and shadows from its flickering flames stretched across the cold earth surrounding the encampment. The occasional pop from fire-consumed branches was the only sound to occupy the sleeping party as they lay unmoving near the roiling blaze. Snoring and occasional slumbering gibberish from their fatigued sleep came from the covered shapes as the companions sought the protection and warmth of the fire while they slept.

Kristian and Erik stood together on the edge of the light, their eyes scouring the darkness for any sign of the Keelut. Nodding to Kristian and patting him on the shoulder, Erik trudged away to the other side of the conflagration as he paced around the camp in a protective arc.

Kristian was left alone with his thoughts as he stared over the meadow, a place that became spookier the more he tried to see and identify each dark object in the dim starlight. As he focused into the darkness, standing alone and facing God knew what, his thoughts ran through his life, hoping to find some peace for the moment as he considered who and what were most important to him.

Turning around and glancing across the fire, Kristian looked at the outline of his father facing away and keeping watch. He thought for a moment how lucky he was to have Erik, and despite devils or not enough food or his broken heart, he knew that the world would always be in proper order if his father was there to back him up. For a brief moment, the notion came to him that he could lose Erik at any moment to the abomination that stalked them, and Kristian realized without hesitation that if that was to happen, his life would immediately lose much of its purpose.

A hand touched him from the side, and Kristian almost jumped as he spun and looked down to see Sigri. She appeared tired, but she looked up at him with probing eyes, as if she had awakened to come and interrogate him at this late time of night. For what reason, Kristian had no idea, but even in her grimy state in the pale light of the fire, her beauty made his breath catch in surprise. He quickly looked away to avoid admitting his continued attraction to her.

"I thought we could talk," said Sigri, and she kept her voice low to avoid attention. "We never had much of a chance since…"

Kristian looked away, even as a pained expression crossed his face. Breathing deep, he finally gazed down and met her eyes. "You never gave me a chance to."

Sigri slowly shook her head, not knowing quite where to start. "What could I say? What can I say? My father arranged the marriage—."

"You think I'm stupid, Sigri?" asked Kristian, interrupting her and raising his voice a bit. He moved his eyes away again, finding the flames of the campfire less painful to look into. "The law is clear, you have to agree to be wedded—it's not up to your father. Never has been."

Sigri nodded, then reached up and moved his face to meet her gaze again. "You're right, but what other choice do I have? We manage a poor life here, and I have to think about my family…"

"You're thinking only about you, not your father or anyone else. What about our times together? What about your promise? I told you I would never find another…"

Tears filled Kristian's eyes as he continued to look down at Sigri. Her features were concerned, but he also saw that they weren't based on similar emotions to his own. With great difficulty, he managed to avoid letting the tears escape as he breathed to control himself.

"I don't know what anything is worth right now," said Kristian, and his tone dropped in concert with his voice cracking, just enough to make him look even more forlorn in the firelight. "Even without this evil around us, I can't much think of anything else. I…don't want a future without you."

Deeply saddened, Sigri dropped her gaze. "You'll find a way. The world is full of other women who would be happy with you. You'll make a great husband—."

"Can't you stop it? Can't we start again? You could ask to have the marriage annulled? Father Galmand will understand. We can make a life together…like we promised."

Trying to be gentle, Sigri shook her head and looked kindly into Erik's pained eyes. "You will always be important to me, you know that, but I can't…won't…go back on my word. What kind of person would I be to break my promise before God? I have a life to make with my husband."

For a moment, Kristian's eyes locked in terror. Unlike with the sword or the claw in combat, the words of a love lost and being spurned were not something he could evade or strike back against. All that was left was to deal with the cold reality that she simply didn't feel for him in the same way, and she probably never had.

Her old professions of love were the promises of a carefree youth that so often were dashed against the rock of the firm and real world. He saw that now in a very obvious way, and although the truth was brutal and utterly depressing, he realized that he was now completely broken. With no pride or self-confidence, his hope for true love was completely shattered.

Somehow that made Kristian understand deep inside that to build something new, sometimes the past must be utterly destroyed and burned away. He felt worse than he ever had in his life, but from now on, he would be a different person to Sigri, his father, and basically everyone. Without absurd and unattainable dreams to cling to, Kristian felt at that moment the old boy within him was now gone forever, lost in the ramblings and unrealistic desires of his childish notions.

Nodding grimly, Kristian pulled away from Sigri. He didn't know if he could hold back his sorrow, but he couldn't deal with looking at the raw pity on her face any longer. He strode away for a half-circle of the fire, making sure to do his guard duty without having to look at his beautiful former love.

"Kristian," Sigri said, her voice shallow in the empty night. "Can't we…?"

With no answer forthcoming, Sigri's voice drifted off, and she looked down at her hands, flexing them in a nervous manner. Unhappy, she returned to her bedroll and laid down, pulling a bearskin over herself and falling into her self-contained thoughts.

Next to Sigri, a wide-awake Rand sat up and watched her irregular breaths move her covering. Rand's expression in the firelight was not of anger or frustration, but instead, the face of a concerned father.

To the other side of the campfire, another father watched with the same features, except for Erik, it was with the abject worry of a doting parent for his deeply distraught son.

# Chapter Thirteen

Two days later, the party made their way on a trail through a remote green meadow. The supply of forage for animals to either side of the path was unusual for Greenland, as it showed the area to be an attractive sub-climate for the grazing of animals. The companions were getting close to the Western Settlement, and this prime land indicated a premium location for upcoming farms as they approached the exterior borders of the secluded village.

Ahead, the trail ascended a long ridge, cresting a few hundred yards from their location and then disappearing over the edge. Far into the background, snow-capped peaks and the jagged outlines of mountains were just visible behind low-lying banks of fog. As those misty wisps of clouds churned ahead from the west with streams of arctic air, it appeared as if the party was advancing into some unnameable and forbidding future, one that threatened to swallow them whole.

Directly above, the sky was covered by overcast weather conditions, and little light penetrated the wide canopy of gray cloud cover, making the location seem dreary—despite it being early in the day. It seemed as if nature itself was rising up to consume their expedition, as if it was not just their wicked and dangerous foe that was intent on destroying their journey of self-preservation.

Erik was first in line as they ascended the trail in single file. Using a crude walking stick fashioned from driftwood, he leaned into the frigid wind as he struggled up the steep path. Behind him, the rest of the group was spread out in a meandering column. Using their spears to steady themselves, they also plodded forward, breathing in rough gasps as they matched Erik's strenuous efforts to move quickly up the rocky grade.

When Erik got to the top of the trail, he stopped in shock as he looked down at the unseen area below. It took several more minutes for the group to catch up with him, and each additional person halted at his side when they reached the same point. One by one, they scanned the area below, and none appeared pleased with what they saw.

Squinting to see into the dim distance, each traveler looked to the valley below, puzzling over the dots of a dozen sheep lying across the sloping green grassland to the side of their path. Unfortunately, the sheep were in clumps and sprawled oddly across the ground, their unmoving bodies positioned at strange angles. Worse, even at the limit of visibility, it was apparent their white wool coats were splotched in blood, showing they were dead where they lay.

"What in God's…?" asked Erik to nobody in particular, and he began to move down the path, eventually branching off from the trail to stride towards the first of the unmoving sheep.

Coming to the first group of three animals, the party spread out around the creatures, staring down with looks of fear and concern. It was a good sign that a flock of sheep showed they were getting close to their goal, but finding livestock that were disemboweled and partially eaten was not a good omen for what was to come next. The guts of the animals were torn out and spread around them, and unlike Father Sturlesson, the slashes into their bodies were savage, with little thought to cleanly extricate their insides.

Sigmar extended his hand to touch one of the sheep. The blood-matted wool showed the wounds to be relatively fresh, with only a day or two between their occurrence and being found.

"They've all been gutted. Never seen something like this," said Sigmar, and he blanched at the waste of meat that would have been a blessing for the party's home village. "These gotta be from the Western Settlement. Who'd slaughter them like this?"

Rand stepped forward, motioning North to the nearest snow and the vague location of the Inuit. "Maybe it was the people native to the snow?"

Standing back from the slaughtered animals, Erik shook his head in irritation. "Not possible. It's true Iqiak's people don't have the same ideas about what's private and what's for public use, but they would never leave meat to rot."

Stepping closer, Kristian knelt next to another of the dead sheep, examining the jagged and vicious cuts. Obviously frustrated, he ran his hand through his unkempt hair, then scowled and pointed to the trail they were using. "Us standing here and worrying isn't going to get any answers. We know exactly what did this. Let's get moving while we still have a long day. We have to get across that last valley before we get to the settlement."

Standing, Kristian walked back toward the trail, not waiting to see who followed. When he walked by Sigri, he didn't smile at her or even raise an eye in recognition. He was clearly ignoring her and didn't care if she noticed. Sigri's face, formerly hopeful, froze in sudden disappointment.

Behind him, the rest of the party looked surprised, wondering with open eyes who this new person was that just replaced the shy Kristian they had all come to know so well.

#

Thorstein's office was busy in the late afternoon. Light shone through the windows, illuminating packing containers mixed with his furniture and personal possessions. Stacked orderly throughout the room, everything was in proper order in an effort to empty the house of all its valuables.

Several workmen and maids hustled around the area, picking up possessions and gently packing them for Thorstein's upcoming move. Each of the men and women who worked for him had concerned faces, with dread and fear coloring their perceptions for the near future of their village and personal families.

Thorstein sat at his wooden desk, working on his ledger and accounting papers, all to ensure preparations were in order for the haul of his goods aboard ships. Checking the numbers and dispositions of not just his personal things, but also his possessions in some of the remaining warehouses, his eyes moved from column to column with the consummate care of a man who doesn't miss a thing when it comes to categorizing and tracking important supplies.

Two servants, Jon and Baldwin, both of advancing age and worried features, moved into the room and set down a large wooden crate. They both looked up expectantly, their gazes locking on Thorstein.

Thorstein nodded politely and gestured to the large crate. "Thank you. Please ensure everything is packed up—immediately. I want the ships loaded as soon as they arrive. Time is of the essence."

Jon nodded and departed the room, moving to another part of the house to collect items to pack. Staying behind, Baldwin lingered, his weary face shy and somewhat uncomfortable.

"What is it?" asked Thorstein, and he focused on the man, obviously not used to engaging his underlings in idle chatter.

"Sigur hasn't come to work for two days," replied Baldwin, and his wrinkly features struck an odd pose of concern, like he had thought long and hard before reporting this to Thorstein. "He lives at one of the outer farms…we're worried about him."

Raising an eyebrow, Thorstein sat up in his chair. "That doesn't sound like him, he's never avoided his duties before. After your work is completed, go to him. Tell him if he wishes to be paid, he has to do the work. No exceptions."

Baldwin nodded slowly in response, then frowned and hesitated.

"What else?" asked Thorstein

"There's others in the village that are missing…not where they're supposed to be. The blacksmith, one of the vendors, the mill operator…people are scared."

Intrigued, Thorstein laced his fingers behind his head and leaned back. After considering Baldwin's information, he stood and walked to the window, where he looked down the dock toward his warehouse storage area.

Out on the wooden dock, many of his personal things had already been carried and were being moved into the warehouses. In time, these things would fetch an excellent price in Iceland, particularly because many of these goods would not be seen again in the markets—rare baubles always made money, at least if he could find the right buyers. He had hoped for the hunting expedition to be winding down, thus allowing for his ships to arrive to aid their escape from this freezing place.

Iceland itself was also cold, but it also was stable there. It had been settled by Vikings in the last part of the ninth century, so for a century or more than Greenland, but in truth, the landholders, wealthy chieftains, and merchants like himself were thriving in comparison to the destitute Norse in this settlement. In fact, he did not know the exact figures, but there must be at least tens of thousands of inhabitants in his island home, which was a big difference from the dwindling several hundred that made their difficult life here.

If Thorstein had not met Sigri and fallen in love with her beauty and inner strength, it was very likely he would have pulled out from this area sooner, and because nobody else at this time cared about Greenland, they would have to adapt to this frozen place without the benefit of regular, or in fact any, trade. He didn't envy people like his hard-working servants, who would have to find a way to survive through these cold winters, but he was a merchant—not a sympathetic clergyman forced to offer alms to the poor.

However, Thorstein did understand he needed to bring Sigri around to his way of thinking, and that would require him to make some effort to mitigate the trauma affecting these poor people. He supposed he could also fit a few of them on board his loaded ships, so perhaps the priest and a few others could be stuffed into his cargo holds for the trip back. This was definitely not the case with Sigri's former lover or his father, though; they would certainly not be welcome in that regard. In fact, if Thorstein had it his way, he would have them thrown overboard halfway home.

Thorstein's mind stopped for a moment as he mulled that thought over. Well…no, he wouldn't do that, he really wasn't that type of man, but neither would he spend any effort to help the backward Erik and Kristian, no matter what Sigri might say.

Shaking his head at this inconvenient situation, Thorstein began talking without looking back at Baldwin. "They must be holed up because of these…troubles. Get the rest of the men together, and we shall go looking for them together, farm-to-farm. Whatever is wrong, we cannot let fear dictate our lives."

Looking relieved, Baldwin nodded and turned away. He paced from the room in a hurry, appearing glad for the support of Thorstein.

When Baldwin was gone, Thorstein's bravado seemed to melt away as he looked quizzically around. Suddenly in a hurry, he collected several books and personal supplies and dropped them in a crate, preparing for departure with little regard compared to his prior obsession with order or planning.

#

There was still some sunlight in the day, but the easy time for travel in the lessening light was fast coming to an end. The path across the last of the valleys near the upcoming settlement was precipitous and worrisome, offering a darkening and forbidding view of this primordial and barely inhabited land.

The cramped and stone-covered trail rose alongside a sheer cliff wall, moving up the expansive canyon as its narrow confines twisted between slick ice and loose rocks.

The party was arranged as it was before, with Erik gingerly picking his way forward, while the rest of the party trailed after and tried to match his exact footsteps to ensure their footing was firm. Every few paces, Erik looked back, ensuring that each of his fellow travelers followed his lead precisely.

The way forward was not for the faint of heart, and a drop of several hundred feet awaited the wrong step if a person should stumble on the slippery face of scattered stones that populated the trails' surface. Each person looked warily from the cliff face, taking in the view with the mental context of the certain death it would provide, instead of the majestic view the precipice offered of distant ice floes and slabs of pointed rocks.

Coming to the narrowest point, each companion carefully skirted an outcropping of rock as they grabbed handholds while moving past. The treacherous move led each of them to breathe deep and focus on every grasp of their hands to ensure their next move would not be their last.

Niels was the last to pass this point, and he breathed deep with relief when he managed to surpass the edge of a rock that was most narrow and fraught with danger.

As he got his footing and silently thanked the Lord for his safe passage, a blurry movement came from the top of the boulder he had just moved by. The Keelut, perched on that huge stone above the point they had all just struggled past, dematerialized from his camouflaged place among the rocky background. Its dark eyes focused down on the last member of the group.

With a silent rush forward, the creature grabbed Niels and flung him off the trail. Surprised, Niels screamed and pinwheeled his arms as he dropped over the edge. His death cry was cut short after a moment as he thudded into the side of the cliff, his body flipping over and over as it crashed into jagged stones and crunched into the rocky earth far below.

With little time to respond, Galmand could barely react when the Keelut rushed forward and grabbed him around the lower leg, burying its claws deep within his calf's chubby flesh. The creature began dragging him away while the priest wailed in agony. Pulling on the screaming man, the powerful being yanked Galmand's ample frame with ease, and the scene had the appearance of a naughty child being dragged to an ignominious bedtime without the benefit of dinner.

Next in line, Sigmar spun around and yelled back in a strident voice. "Father, hang on."

As Sigmar rushed down the trail to advance on their attacker, the Keelut produced a small and shiny black stone in its off-hand. Rearing back, it threw the missile at Sigmar with frightening speed. There was a sickening crack, and Sigmar stumbled and fell, not even breaking his fall as he collapsed face-down onto the constricted pathway.

Next came Kristian, who stumbled past Sigmar's still form and moved to help Galmand. Drawing his knife, he held up the ancient blade as he faced the Keelut for the second time in his young life. Strangely, Kristian was unafraid, and the creature's eyes moved to his weapon, recognizing that it presented some unknowable danger to it.

Keeping his claws in Galmand, the Keelut was still focused on Kristian, and it did not notice the clergyman's struggles below. Reaching up, Galmand wrapped one of his priestly stoles around the monster's arm. The vestment had several embroidered crosses on it, and when it was affixed around the creature's limb, a fierce hissing emanated from it.

The Keelut screamed an inhuman cry at the burning sound, and it pulled back from Galmand, letting his bloody leg fall to the ground. Stepping back, the surprised creature's whitish flesh was covered in boils and scorched from contact with the holy cloth.

From further up the trail, Erik struggled to make his way back, moving past the suddenly dumbfounded others as they stared open-mouthed. Yelling between panicked gasps for breath, he pushed Rand and Sigri aside, rushing as carefully as he dared on the narrow cliff. "I'm coming Kristian, wait for me."

Stopping itself, the beast looked down at Galmand, then up to Kristan and Erik. For a moment, it appeared indecisive, not knowing what to do in the face of such determined resistance.

Galmand took the moment to crawl away from the Keelut, gasping in terror as he tried to put distance between them.

Moving with unnatural agility, the Keelut bounded up the sheer wall to the side of the trail, its claws easily finding purchase in the rocks as it seemed to ignore gravity. In a moment, it was gone, disappearing into the mountain's shadows as it climbed away from the shocked party.

#

Sigmar lay on his side, his bulky and sprawled form unmoving on the cold ground. His right eye, lifeless and staring at something far past this world, looked out over the silent valley. The black stone thrown by the Keelut was buried deep into his face, below the other eye, and was lodged so far in that the rest of his features were malformed around it. The grievous effect of the wound meant the entirety of his face was swollen, and even with his distinctive shaggy beard, it was difficult to easily determine who he formerly was.

To his side, Ketil knelt over his friend, patting the dead man on the shoulder, as if Sigmar might soon awaken and rejoin the expedition. Few men in the world were more gruff or hard than Ketil, but at that moment, he sobbed like a mourning boy who had lost all his childhood friends in one traumatic event.

Farther down the trail, Galmand moaned in pain, holding onto his seriously wounded calf. Sigri had tied a bandage around the injury to stop the bleeding, but the throbbing pain wasn't reduced by the application of her dressing. At a place where medicines were few and far between, he was going to have to endure the continuous and sharp ache from the wound in his mangled muscle.

Sigri stared down at Galmand, pitying the priest in his injured state and offering him a supportive smile. Galmand didn't seem to care at the moment, and he breathed deep as he tried to come to terms with the agony coursing through his leg.

Shuffling up next to his daughter, Rand nodded down to the priest, then embraced Sigri in a show of worry at the entire state of their struggling group. For some time, he held her like that, clinging to his daughter as the most important thing in the world.

Hugging Rand back, Sigri spoke softly, but she was plenty loud for all the other survivors to hear. "What…now?"

With his back to the cliff wall, Erik stood watch over the group, looking around intently for their otherworldly stalker. Walking to the edge of the trail, he peered far down to the crumpled form of Niels, whose broken body was shattered and bled-out at the bottom of the gorge. Stepping back, he ran his hands over his wrinkly and unwashed face before answering. "We get moving. Now, before it comes back."

Kristian, standing guard farther down the trail, agreed to that sentiment with a grunt. Walking forward, he leaned down and offered the portly Galmand his arm for support. Grimacing, the cleric nodded and managed to struggle to his feet over several long moments of painful exertions. Without another word,

Galmand leaned into Kristian, and they struggled up the trail, moving as quickly as the priest's maimed condition would allow.

Looking unsure of themselves, Sigri and Rand met eyes and soon followed.

Left with his friend's corpse, Ketil stayed where he was, continuing to pat his decades-long compatriot affectionately. Erik moved over to the large man, placing his hand on Ketil's shoulder in a show of support.

With an anguished face, Ketil acquiesced to the need to leave, and after another moment, he rose and collected himself. Wiping away his tears, he nodded at Erik and stalked up the trail after the others.

Erik watched Ketil walk away, his eyes pained and his heart heavy. Taking a deep breath, he looked down at Sigmar's body as he prepared to follow. Focusing on the massive wound to his face, Erik became curious as he thought about what had killed the man.

Bending down, Erik traced where the object had been lodged in the facial flesh. Thinking for a moment, he pulled out a knife and probed the gory edges of the wound. Inserting the blade deeper, he managed to pry the dark stone from its place far within Sigmar's skull. Holding the strange stone up in the waning light, he focused on its bizarre color and odd weight as he ran it between his fingers.

Taking out a piece of cloth, Erik wiped the blood from the stone and his fingers. Then, he tucked the missile into a pouch inside his filthy shirt.

After Sigmar's years of service to the village, after all he had done to keep the peace and lend a hand when it was needed, his destiny was to be left to rot in some far-off place at the end of the world. Not only was it unfair, but it was also a revolting way to treat a fallen friend, and Erik was ashamed to allow it to happen.

But, Erik was a practical man. If he wanted to join Sigmar in the afterlife, or worse, see his son join him in early death, the most certain way for that to happen was to stand around and wait for their turn at a violent end from their horrid foe. The Keelut was chasing them all across Greenland, and true to its apparently demonic nature, it was not going to stop until they were all dead. To escape or to kill it outright, assuming it could be killed, was their only way forward.

Sighing, Erik patted his faithful friend on the arm a final time. Grimly, he stood and set out to catch up with the shrinking number of people remaining in their wayward hunting party.

# Chapter Fourteen

The clacking of the horses' hooves on the cobblestoned streets of the Eastern Settlement were the loudest sounds to be heard in the afternoon's overcast and windy environment. Groups of people, pale and with fearful eyes, looked up to watch the procession of riders make its way through the central square of the old and diminutive village. Filthy children dressed in disused rags scurried out of the way as the retinue of horses gently swerved around abandoned market stalls and untended wooden buildings.

From atop the most beautiful and healthy horse, Thorstein nodded toward the unhappy and hope-starved faces of the villagers. "I never saw such dispirited people. They look as if they are waiting for their end, like sheep to a slaughter."

To his side, Baldwin leaned forward on his own horse, nodding sadly. "I can't say I blame them. They've been facing starvation, and now…something more."

Bringing his horse to a stop, Thorstein brought the animal about and scanned around the village's people and buildings. After considering their current predicament, he looked at both Jon and Baldwin with a depressed huff of his well-tended features. "What is the status of the missing?"

Baldwin moved his eyes down from his employer, like he didn't want to talk about what was clearly a bad situation. "We haven't gotten to every farm yet, but it isn't good. There's fifteen people missing, and blood at each of their houses—but no bodies. It's like hell has come and is dragging them away."

From the other side of Thorstein, Jon chimed in with a voice that bordered on hysterical. "And those that still live won't come out to talk with us. They're afraid we're there to do 'em harm. Everything is wrong, nobody trusts anyone else."

There was silence for a time, and Thorstein's expression went from worried to fearful as he contemplated what was happening. He moved his eyes from one villager to another, taking in their desperation and hopelessness with a detached sadness, like he was watching a seal on the ice that was soon to be killed and eaten by a ravenous bear.

Looking over to a tawdry porch, Thorstein saw a grimy young boy and girl staring up at him from the shadows of a drooping overhang. Their eyes locked on him in the scared way of children when they are unprotected and facing the unknown. Such empty and innocent expressions were the very definition of irretrievable and unfair sadness.

Thorstein saw that no parents were around them now, and he realized it didn't take an erudite genius to figure out that they might not have any. For once in a very long time, a pang of conscience rang its distant bell in his head, and he felt genuine pity for the children. For a man like Thorstein, that was a revelation of sorts, and he looked away before the feeling overwhelmed him.

Spinning his horse around, many more thoughts crossed Thorstein's mind, and he took in the rest of the dreary faces and sorrowful conditions that filled the village. It seemed the whole world was looking at him, and for once, he started to care what their destitute expressions conveyed.

Though not an emotional person by nature, being witness to this misery suddenly held some value in Thorstein's eternally selfish mind. All his life, he had made deals and consummated transactions with forthrightness in his actions; he had never overtly cheated anyone in his business matters, and he worked to keep his name and reputation spotless above all else. He had always thought himself a good and upright person, so long as the terms of the deal were spelled out and signed in an open manner.

But this was something else, and like a blind man that suddenly sees when a lifetime of darkness is lifted away, he processed what really lay before him: people that had nothing and faced certain death—if nobody was there to fight for him.

This wasn't about the idea of furthering wealth or prestige, it was about something more, something that tickled at notions of life and the purpose for mankind's very goals on this wide and brutal earth. His love for Sigri had pushed away his self-important thoughts, replacing them with a promise of something better to be gleaned from existence. But these poor, suffering peasants had done even more, finally awakening something else inside Thorstein: a desire to live for someone else and to risk something more than money for once in his life.

Thinking harder and harder, Thorstein's mind worked on the problem. Sitting erect on his horse, he was now like the central character in some important play, and the anxious crowd waited for him to deliver his vitally important lines.

Breathing deep, Thorstein raised his voice to a shout, so that all who were present could hear. He started haltingly, but as his tone increased, the conviction in his voice became more obvious as his commitment hardened. "Alright…get all the able-bodied men. All the children and women. Bring any weapons you have and all the food that you have left. Come to the main warehouse, that is my…our…biggest building. Whatever is after us, we will only survive if we stand together."

Spinning to Jon, Thorstein pointed at the man, and before he talked, he saw something there he hadn't witnessed before in his humble servant: hope.

Lowering his tone, he spoke pointedly, making sure his intent was clear and that the gravity of his words was communicated without error. "And go to every farm. All of them. Tell them, that to stay where they are means certain death.

Ask them to join us…implore them to come. It is their last chance."

As Jon took in his words, he forced a grin around his rotten teeth. Nodding eagerly, he motioned to the other men on horses behind him. Kicking into a gallop, they departed with a rush out of the village and into the farms beyond, gone on their mission of mercy to save their neighbors.

Turning around, Thorstein peered over to Baldwin, who also allowed a smile to greet his boss. Moving his gaze back to the porch with the children, Thorstein was happy to see an emerging grin from the bedraggled boy and girl.

Thorstein smiled over at them in turn, and for once, the show of kindness was not forced.

#

Erik leaned down and squinted, staring across the frost-tinged fields of a large and empty Norse farm. His face was full of anxious doubt, and he moved his eyes around uncertainly, looking for something in the closing light of day.

Kristian crouched at Erik's side, his face also a mask of worry and indecision. He glanced over at his father, scrunching his face in exasperation at what he saw. Neither looked happy with what lay amongst the descending shadows before them.

Ahead, the open fields of the wide-ranging homestead were studded with dilapidated fences and wooden troughs for holding water. Several tools were scattered and leaned against the posts of contained corrals, while formerly extensive gardens were downtrodden and looked abandoned by whoever had lived here in the recent past.

A series of shoddy barns surrounded a larger main house, a place that was almost hidden under its overgrown turf roof. The faint howl of a wind gust made the empty setting seem haunted and lonely, even more than was usually the case in such rural areas.

Looking specifically at the desolate fields, Erik peered at the remains of several cows and sheep that lay lifelessly across the matted grass. Their numerous hideous wounds and bloody condition indicated they suffered the same fate as the poor animals near the trail they just descended.

Standing behind Erik and Kristian was the rest of the party, and nobody seemed optimistic while peering at the surroundings. Rand scowled at the apparently abandoned farm, while Ketil surveyed the scene with the stark expression of someone who would believe anything at this point. The other members wore the dull and apathetic features of people that were getting accustomed to misery and bad news.

Death and unending hardship had a way of making people grow colder in order to deal with their environment, and in the case of these travelers, this acquired coldness found expression in their weary eyes and downtrodden frowns.

Whispering, Erik motioned to the whole area, as if keeping his voice quiet served a valid purpose. "Just like the others. You think all of them were killed?"

There wasn't an immediate answer to the question, and Kristian looked over to his father with a knowing and sarcastic grimace. *Where else would they be?*

Breaking free from the limited cover of the few trees they stood amongst, Galmand hopped out on a makeshift crutch as he swept the farm with a curious gaze. Everyone looked to him as if he should be more discreet in his movements, but the priest was unworried about being seen.

"The devil that did this must know where we are," Galmand said, speaking loudly to address their concerns. "It is difficult to see the benefit of sneaking around at this point."

The other companions listened with unconvinced faces. After a moment of silence, Erik agreed with a shrug and walked over to Galmand. Standing next to the wounded man, he motioned for the others to join them.

When all the group was detached from the tree line and were milling about, Galmand spoke again. "I think we can see why Father Sturlesson was on his way to our settlement. And…why he never made it."

Nodding, Erik looked to the main house, focusing on it as if he still expected someone to come out and greet them. "I never knew a tougher man in my life than Ungertoq," he said, referring to the chieftain and the owner of the farm where they now stood. "He could wrestle a bear, literally."

No response came from the others. Moving forward, Galmand grunted from the lancing pain in his leg and began hopping toward the main house. His plodding pace was slow, yet he remained determined to make it on his own as he ambled with his crutch across the empty pasture.

Erik and the rest walked after the priest, taking their time to scan the area for any more signs of their wretched enemy. As they got close to the home, they passed the large form of an immense bull lying dead to the side, its awkward head pointing down with its enormous horns half-buried in the rough soil.

#

Ungertok's main living area was practical and attractive, combining sturdy wooden furniture with simple carvings of arctic animals. On the main inner wall, above a soot-filled hearth, was an ancient coat-of-arms on an immense oak shield, showing an old-style Norse set of axes crossed together over a faded black background.

Above the shield, in a sign that portended badly for the home's occupants, there were two blank spaces where swords had once been. The rest of the area was normal, with typical household goods such as a trunk and some cabinets. A sheen of collected dust covered the surface of the room's furnishings, showing the place to have been unoccupied for some time.

Several of the companions sat around a long feasting table. Open sacks of food lay on its grainy surface, and Erik, Galmand, Sigri, and Rand munched on hunks of dried meat and hard bread as they looked curiously around. Kristian stood to the side, peering at crude paintings on the exterior walls.

Glancing up, Erik stared at the spot where Ungertok's swords had hung, and the discolored area on the wall where they had been displayed showed the swords had been merely ornamental and unused for a long time. If there had been a sudden need for the blades to be pressed into service on short notice, it wasn't a fortuitous sign for finding Ungertok and his family.

Looking down, Erik frowned at yet another wound to his heart because of another lost friend. He had met the outrageous and entertaining Ungertoq a decade before, and each time Erik saw him on these hunting trips, he had liked the rowdy man progressively more.

As a host, Ungertoq had been magnanimous and pleasant, wrapping his gargantuan arms around Erik in a crushing hug, then drinking the rest of the trip away in the smiling presence of his followers while Erik enjoyed the leader's hospitality. Ungertoq was respected, liked and feared by all, and nobody earthly would try to harm him—at least anyone of sane mind or with intentions for a long life.

Erik caught himself smiling at the thought, and deep inside, he hoped the Keelut was not the reason for the man's disappearance. He even imagined for a moment that the boastful and happy chieftain would burst in at any time to greet them, holding a party until deep in the night in honor of all his guests, just like they always had. But, given the circumstances and the ferocity of the Keelut, he considered that to be as likely as a fleet of heavenly ships arriving from above and saving all the Greenlanders in some divine show of God's love.

Peering down at his clenched hands, Erik realized that was the problem with grief and getting past the deaths of those he cared about. The trauma of missing someone always made him feel like they were still there, just around the corner, waiting to be seen by Erik's hungry eyes. Be they Sigmar, Ungertoq, a score of friends he'd lost over the years, or his long-dead and loving wife, he still felt like those people were there, ready to enjoy those moments together in the funny way they had always done before.

The processing of memories had always been a strange thing to Erik because for him, the past was almost a living thing, a place where if he thought about it hard and long enough, he felt like he was physically there. Grimacing, he wondered why God let you remember your loved ones so well, even when their bodies were long buried and decayed.

Looking reflexively over to Kristian, Erik caught his son smiling and looking at some gaudy painting on Ungertoq's wall, a simple piece of horrible art that showed a waterfall flowing into a raging river. A smile crossed Erik's own lips at the badly painted image, and it hit him just then why he could remember his loved ones so well: *Because it makes everything matter.*

From the unseen back room of the house, a pacifying tone came from Ketil, and the man was obviously defensive as he raised his voice. "I'm not trying to hurt ye. Take it easy."

From the back hallway, Nunik emerged. Tired and dirty, the young Inuit daughter was also feisty and fierce-eyed. She held a spear towards the back room as she backed out of the dark portion of the bedroom area.

Ketil followed her out, keeping his arms and hands away from his weapons. He glanced at the rest of the party, sounding frustrated. "I told 'er, we're friends. I hope she agrees to be, anyway—we sure need the help."

Scanning the rest of the room, Nunik swirled to face each of the newcomers. She stared suspiciously as she gazed at each member of the group, like they all were there to do her harm. When she got to Kristian, though, her features softened as her dark eyes locked on his.

Lowering the point of her weapon but keeping her defensive pose, Nunik's words were easy to understand, even in her tribe's peculiar accent. "Where are others that lived here, and who are you?"

#

Later, the entire hunting party stood around the same feasting table, where they stared expectantly down at Nunik. Intrigued, Kristian leaned forward and peered at her with particular interest, showing her a grin that implied more than idle kindness. Reaching into his cloak, he produced a linen-wrapped hunk of food and offered it to her with a bashful smile.

Visibly hungry, Nunik accepted without hesitation. She began gnawing on the piece of seal, showing no regard for formal manners as she tore off and munched on the tough flesh. Her face blushed eagerly while she consumed the simple food, as if it was the most delectable sustenance she ever had the pleasure to eat. Kristian nodded with satisfaction as she finished the impromptu meal, then followed it up with a swig of water from his offered animal skin.

When she was done, Nunik wiped her mouth absently and picked at some gristle caught in her immaculate white teeth. Even with the gesture, she was striking in her beauty, with pronounced cheekbones and dark eyes that coursed with a wild spirit for living.

Nunik was the type of person that others would remember as intense and interesting, even if she said nothing during a nameless encounter. Such liveliness of spirit was rare enough that when it was found, either from newly met tribe members or the occasional Norseman, the result was a lasting impression of her as exciting or alluring.

Sighing, Nunik scanned the rest of the room, focusing on the various hunters and trying to figure out who exactly was in charge.

Leaning on the table with his hands, Rand looked down at Nunik with sympathetic eyes. "The beast took your parents? Why didn't you flee to your people?"

Licking her fingers, Nunik responded in a monotone voice, like her reason should be self-evident. "I went away from my tribe. I did not want to lead demon to my people. I hoped to find help here—we have good relationship with this chief."

Nunik motioned to the house around them, obviously unhappy that Ungertoq was not here to help. The others were equally unhappy he was missing and nodded in pained agreement at the emptiness of the home without its lively owner.

It became quiet, and Nunik and Kristian made eye contact several more times. Everyone noticed the youthful attraction between them, including Erik and Sigri. Erik was delighted by the spectacle of a new interest for his son, but Sigri frowned at the overt display of attention from her former lover to this strange new woman.

"You did not wish to lead them to your people?" asked Sigri, her tone skeptical. "But this town of innocents was easy for you to endanger?"

Nunik shrugged, apparently still comfortable with her prior decision to come here. The Inuit woman was young, barely of the age of womanhood, but her bearing was unshakable. "My people are few and scattered over ice. Yours are much more numerous. I thought you could kill what followed me easier. This was my thinking…but when I arrived, all village was empty. I found nobody here or in other farms. Only a donkey lived in a nearby barn."

Erik cleared his throat and shook his head, directing a grouchy glance at Sigri. "The girl isn't to blame for this, any more than we are."

Looking back to Nunik, Erik spoke with an empathetic tone as he continued. "You said your father was a shaman?"

Nunik nodded. Her demeanor was tough, but her eyes teared up at the mention of her slain father, Tonraq. Life for the Inuit could be brutal and short, but their appreciation for family was no less intense than the Norse. The loss of both parents was a heavy weight for her to bear, no matter how worldly and resilient she was.

Grunting, Galmand sat down and propped his wounded leg on a bench. Smiling politely to Nunik, he lent his own kindhearted voice to the discussion. "And so, this demon continues his spiritual harvest. More victims of its wicked evil. I will say a prayer for your parents, and you can hope that they now dwell in the home of our Lord and Savior."

Nunik nodded in appreciation at the words of the priest, but she otherwise stayed silent. Caught in the early stage of grief, she undoubtedly would process their tragic deaths for a substantial time.

Pulling at his uneven whiskers, Erik huffed and started to pace the room. Taking each step deliberatively, he ran a hand over his greasy and graying hair. "And so it seems half of our people in Greenland, and all who were in this settlement, are now dead. We've got to come up with a plan, find a way to survive. There's got to be a way to fight this devil."

Shaking his head, Rand gestured to the blank spaces on the wall above the shield. "I'm not sure we can. As you've said, Erik,

Ungertoq was our most dangerous fighter, and even he seems to have failed to stop it."

Trying to recline on the hardwood chair and find a comfortable position for his leg, Galmand chuckled humorlessly. His voice rose in that way it often did when he was about to give a sermon. "If I could offer some insight, as we face our end and maybe the end of our people…I would like to describe a bit of history. It might give some perspective to our current plight."

When nobody answered, Galmand continued with a thoughtful nod. "Five hundred years ago, our ancestors, the feared Vikings, plundered much of Europe. From Ireland all the way to islands in the sea near the Holy Land, the Norse pillaged, raped, murdered, stole treasure, took slaves…on and on. Good people everywhere were terrified when our people visited their homelands."

"Not nice to hear, Father, and not helpful at the present," Erik said dryly.

Shrugging, Galmand continued with his best wise-man look. "Our people put to death whole communities. Enslaved children and women. We were truly a scourge for those that had to deal with our depredations. How many people in small towns such as ours had this same conversation we're having now, while they feared for their families and places of worship? While they prayed to God for deliverance from the Viking scourge?"

"What you say is true, Father Galmand, certainly," said Rand, furrowing his brow in confusion. "But how does that help us? Are we responsible for our ancestors' deeds? Are you saying it's time for us to pay for their actions?"

Galmand shook his head wryly. "No, of course not; no man is responsible for another's sins. The point is, we have lived here since that time for hundreds of years, and now, we are mostly farmers. All those times of violence and "glory" are long gone. But think of those victims from that distant period. How did they cope? How is it that their descendants have prospered since? My understanding from reading various tomes is that they are doing well in comparison to us."

"They surely fled…or fought if they were able," said Rand, still looking for Galmand's point.

"Precisely," said Galmand. "In our similar moment of sorrow, we now must decide to run away or to fight this menace, even if our pursuer is more dangerous than mere men."

Sigri tilted her head worriedly, unhappy with the thought of losing everything in a hopeless battle with the Keelut. "We have already been to the harbor. There are no more boats to go hunting, and now, it's a dangerous trip home by land, over narrow animal trails, and across treacherous ravines. How do we fight—or run?"

Kristian, quiet until now, stepped forward and dropped his long knife on the table with a clank. His expression was rough, like he was in no mood for retreating, even if it was the smart thing to do. "I saw my father hack off the arm of that thing. I also saw Father Galmand wound it with only his vestments, so it can be harmed, maybe even destroyed. Are we now to run away like children?"

"Not children," replied Sigri, growing annoyed. "You may have also noticed the monster's hacked-off arm had grown back when it attacked us again on the cliff trail. That isn't a normal thing we can fight against. Really, we must focus on our town, to make sure it survives. Our people need us; they will starve without food, and we can't carry much across the mountains back to them."

Stepping near his son, Erik patted Kristian on the shoulder as he met his eyes. There was newfound respect for Kristian in Erik's approving stare, and Erik enthusiastically understood his son's eagerness to fight back, even if it wasn't the best option for their people currently.

Turning to the others, Erik spoke in a diplomatic manner, but it was also clear he was announcing a decision, not a suggestion. "We have to get back to the Eastern Settlement, that's a certainty. From there, we must get on Thorstein's boats, or we're all going to die, including everyone left in the Eastern Settlement. Like Iqiak said, to stay in Greenland is death. Unless we want to live in the same manner as the Inuit, our time here on this immense land is coming to an end."

Erik had just spoken out loud what had been so long considered by the people of Greenland: their end as a people and a culture. Centuries of their life and struggles, happiness and sorrow, and pride in their heritage would be over. Everyone in the room, including Nunik, knew that the only thing certain in life was change, and that all peoples and cultures, big and small, would eventually come to an end. Still, to have it happen in such a direct way was a difficult matter to reflect on, especially for stubborn settlers who had never planned to give up their home.

Taking his cue to soften the blow for this shocking need to abandon their homeland, Galmand spoke gently, raising his gaze to meet each of the assembled travelers. "In the Good Book, it is said that the coming of the Lord, the end of the world, would come "like a thief in the night." I do not know if it pertains to us only in this faraway land, but we can at least be comforted to know that there is a time to abandon what you know in pursuit of something better. The history of the world as we know it, both Christian and secular, is alive with people who must flee to make a more secure future. The devil pursues us, but it cannot be allowed to win."

Rand and Sigri glanced at each other defensively, like they were worried what Thorstein might say to such a planned course of action. Neither was certain Thorstein would be able to give up so much of his collected wealth to save starving peasants. Their worry was not just that he would refuse to do so, but what would happen if such a refusal would occur. Desperate people would do desperate things to survive, and it didn't matter how well armed Thorstein's men and ships were—people would be killed on both sides if bad decisions were made.

After peering at father and daughter with cool eyes, Erik sighed and motioned to Nunik. "You're welcome to come with us, at least until we can find some of your people. Or, farther if you want."

Pulling off his scabbarded sword, Erik set it gently next to Kristian's knife. Looking in a circle from one person to another, he let what he said sink in. Erik was never one for big words or lengthy speeches, but his tone and committed features were convincing. "That's the only way out of this. We'll need to get everyone to Iceland, where they'll have food…and hopefully, no devils. We do what we have to in order to survive. Bravery is always welcomed when facing an enemy, but certain death here is not a good goal for us."

Inhaling, Erik's voice dropped off. Concentrating on the hilt of his sword, sadness overcame his haggard expression. "And maybe someday, we can return to this land. Our…home."

# Chapter Fifteen

Crates of wood were stacked around the main warehouse in a continuous row, providing a defensive line for the assembled Norse villagers. Stacks of assorted refuse, from broken tools to piles of old scrap iron, were braced at odd angles on the outside of the crates, ensuring that any approach to the fortifications would be difficult for prospective attackers to bypass.

Behind the fortifications, the area was bustling with activity. A makeshift corral was formed at the back of the building, with the remaining goats of the settlement standing in groups, looking confused as they munched on hay. Alongside, a village butcher worked with multiple carcasses, chopping into the dwindling herd to harvest meat for the surrounding families and workers.

The sound of nervous laughter mixed with the movement of goods from stressed residents, showing a surprising lightheartedness in the locals' demeanor. Each person carried a spear or pitchfork, indicating their deadly motivation as they prepared to confront their unseen foe.

Inside the warehouse, Thorstein sat at his desk. Attentive, he concentrated on a sheaf of paper, with the lines for defensive fortifications scrawled in bold script below him. The precise dimensions and location of each assorted breastwork showed Thorstein's obsession with numbers and minutia had carried over well to the new task of preparing for the settlement's defense.

Motioning to smaller wooden containers against an interior wall, Thorstein spoke to Baldwin. "Those contain all the dried caribou meat. It should last a while but see to it that the children are fed first. The parents should not be overly concerned about their well-being as they guard the exterior wall."

Baldwin, standing near and looking down at a list of other perishable goods, nodded. "And the barrels of ale?"

Raising his eyes, Thorstein chuckled, his face momentarily amused. "For the parents, later, perhaps—when they are not on the wall. I have never been a military man, but I would suppose we will have to adapt to these dreadful circumstances in the best way possible."

Smiling, Baldwin nodded again and moved to the far side of the building. As he began giving directions to other villagers, Thorstein returned to his quill and paper, where he scrawled a new line on the parchment, planning for a secondary place of retreat if the exterior wall were to be breached by their enemy.

After several more minutes of writing, Thorstein finished and rubbed his eyes. Even though exhausted, his fatigue was also marked by a new commitment, and even the dark circles on his worried face didn't detract from the sense of purpose in his features.

Watching the villagers through the main entrance, Thorstein couldn't help but admire their calm expressions and focused determination as they went about their defensive arrangements. Their lives were built on struggle, and that constant state of striving to endure was the only condition they had ever seemed to know.

"You are the salt of the earth" was a biblical quote that Galmand had mentioned in one of his sermons, referring to the humble people that carried out the important work of the world on a day-to-day basis. Truthfully, Thorstein had never been too fond of thinking about such things. The pronouncements of religion for him had often seemed irrelevant to his life and business. They were not necessarily wrong, just unimportant for how he lived.

And Thorstein had known such people, these working villagers, as a means for increasing his profit or business reach for his entire adult life. They were as the cow in the field or the rabbit rummaging amongst vegetables to him, which is to say they were a part of the world he saw as necessary, but he had not for a second considered their personal well-being or individual struggles. He wasn't hostile to them or their concerns;

they just didn't have any true impact on his thoughts or life, except for what advantage they could get for him.

But something new was being formed in Thorstein's mind as he thought about them now: respect, as well as a sense of brotherhood, especially as everyone's situation here grew more dire. This new-found respect for his fellow man was a strange and intrusive concept, and it tickled Thorstein's mind with a pleasant sensation, one that he didn't yet fully understand—even as he felt exhilarated by it.

Pacing back toward Thorstein, Baldwin set some more papers in front of his boss and spoke in a low voice. "Except for a few people still collecting their animals, I think we're ready. Whoever is attacking us, they won't have an easy time. We just need to wait for the ships."

Looking up, Thorstein's expression grew contemplative. Standing, he walked to the main entrance, where he could see out over the interior of the natural harbor encircling his buildings' positions. Gazing around, he looked over all his stacked, long-accrued possessions and trade goods, things that had taken years from his life to collect or earn. Suddenly, all that effort and all those assorted items didn't seem so important. Impending doom had a way of sharpening the mind as to what actually mattered in life.

Thorstein tilted his head to the side as he considered their defensive design, looking for any weakness that their anonymous enemy could exploit. Looking inland, his eyes scanned the tree line, then gazed over to his abandoned house, that edifice of success that he had so long maintained to show off his wealth. He turned away from that large structure now, suddenly embarrassed to have ever owned it.

"We wait until my wife returns," said Thorstein, and he turned back to Baldwin, his expression grim. "Whatever happens, we wait for her, no matter how long it takes."

#

The hunting companions and their new Inuit visitor lay around the front room of Ungertoq's house. Splayed on the floor among piles of furry blankets and personal supplies, they dozed contentedly, with only a few snores or periodic coughs to interrupt the quiet atmosphere.

A dim oil lamp glowed in the corner, keeping a vague but pleasant hue inside the cramped room.

Standing near the front door, Kristian peered out the window that abutted the entrance. Above, light from the moon slipped through wavy clouds in the night's clear sky, illuminating the abandoned fields of the Norse homestead.

Visibility was good in those chilly pastures, and Kristian's gaze jumped from the husk of one dead animal to another as he visually inspected the remains of the farm's slaughtered animals. Tilting his head, something bothered his mind, and he struggled to understand what nagged at his thoughts from a subconscious level. Something was missing.

As he continued his overwatch, Kristian focused far across the field. His attention came to rest on the line of brush that intermingled with a few trees, forming a dark blur on the periphery of his distant sight. This was the opposite side of the meadow where they had first arrived, and the darkness beyond it ascended a low mountain that was shrouded in the shadows of a dark forest.

There among the bushes, a dense mist began to whirl, forming the same weird and churning coils of fog that they had earlier witnessed before the attack at sea. As if living, the mist again appeared to have its own luminescent tinge, and the vague light within the roiling fog seemed to grow larger as Kristian stared at it.

In time, the fog started to drift onto the open field, as if it was setting out on a course toward the sanctuary where they all slept. As it crept forward, the flowing mass expanded, its simmering confines stretching toward the house.

Growing alarmed, Kristian hustled across the room, gently stepping over Rand as he came to his father's slumbering form. Shaking Erik awake, his spooked voice was loud in the calm area. "Father, something is coming toward us."

Suddenly alert, Erik took only a moment to gather himself. Following Kristian to the window, his gaze followed his son's pointed finger out into the night, where his eyes came to rest on the swirling mist.

It was now halfway across the field, and its speed increased as it came toward them. From their perspective, nothing was visible behind it, and the result was that the wall of clouds was like a dark cover blotting out the rest of their perceivable world.

Pulling the shutter closed, Erik gestured to the other shutter—and for Kristian to close it as well. Turning to the party, Erik's voice boomed through the room, bringing everyone awake with his frantic tone. "Everybody up. Get your weapons, it's coming for us again."

The group responded quickly, scrambling to extricate themselves from their blankets and the light sleep they had been immersed in. In little time, they were up and clear-eyed, staring with terrified worry for what came next. Holding up spears and swords, nobody questioned what was coming, because they saw in Erik's alarmed face that it could only be their endlessly wicked pursuer.

Having closed and barred the other window, the entrance and all openings to the turf-enclosed house were closed. The nature of the Norse structures meant they were built with only one way to enter, and all the party members faced the entry point in agitated expectation.

Erik motioned for Kristian to back up more, leaving extra space to defend themselves when their adversary tried to break through the door. Doing as requested, Kristian stepped back and took his place next to his father. Each held their blades at the ready as they tried to control their breathing and bite back their fear.

In the back of the armed group, Galmand clutched his substantial silver crucifix, clinging to it in hope it would offer safety from what was coming. Licking his quivering lips, he held out the cross, girding himself for the Lord's protection in whispered prayers.

From beyond the door, a distant howling came. It was almost terrestrial, like a dog or wolf, but it also contained an unnatural lamentation, like something that was being forced into existence against its will. Stealing glances at one another, the group's terror-stricken eyes awaited their hideous foe.

From the cracks around the door and windows, the invasive mist began to leak into the room. The whole front of the room started to be obscured with the otherworldly fog, threatening to make visibility non-existent for the companions. The moaning sound from the night outside increased as something got closer to the door.

A huge impact blasted through the entrance, and it was flung off its hinges, splintering wood in all directions. Bursting into the room was an immense bull, fifteen hundred pounds of frightening fury and horrible wails as it charged ahead.

Swinging its crazed head around, it thrashed its sharp horns about, trying to gouge whatever was in its path. Thrusting one sharp horn into Rand's arm, it cast him against the wall, where he thudded against it and crumpled to the floor.

Getting his footing, Kristian moved to attack the rampaging brute, but with a vicious shake of its head, the creature threw him into Erik, and they both slid across the table and crashed into the ground.

"Arghhhh," screamed Ketil, yelling a battle cry as he rushed forward and brought his sword slashing across the raging animal's spine. The blade cleaved through the creature's bones and flesh, but the wild beast turned on Ketil without regard to the severe wound.

Sizing him up, the bull faced Ketil, drawing in great gasps of breath through its dark and fetid snout. The beast's eyes were filmed-over and white, like those of a long-dead corpse. Scratching a hoof on the floor, it prepared to charge.

For a moment, Ketil met those dead eyes with his own fearful gaze, and he seemed to connect with it, like it was some ancient evil recognizing him from within those milky eye sockets. Hesitating, Ketil lost the opportunity to act first and use his better agility to escape the enormous animal.

Crashing forward, the animal drove him back, slamming Ketil against the wall and impaling him on both horns with its jarring power. The entire wall of the house shook from the impact, and Ketil screamed in agony as he chopped down at the uncontrolled strength of the creature.

Stuck fast, Ketil was slung from side to side as the bull shook him, repeatedly bashing his frame against the wall's log surface. Continuing to scream, Ketil plunged his blade into its back, tearing great gashes in its muscled flank.

From the side, Nunik thrust her spear through the bull's side, running it all the way through its thick midsection. Joining her, Sigri, Kristian, and Erik also rammed their blades into the beast, screaming in anger as they plunged their weapons deep into its stout flesh. Again and again, they continued their attacks, maniacally trying to stop the horrible assault on Ketil.

The enraged animal let out a woeful cry and collapsed under the blows, going suddenly quiet. Above it, Nunik and Kristian continued to stick the beast with savage stabs, while Erik moved forward to help Ketil.

Coming to the aid of his large friend, Erik's panicked eyes jerked in fear as he tried to comfort the grievously injured man. "Ketil, you'll make it. I'll get you free, and we'll…"

Ketil's face was covered in his own gore as he spit out blood in great gouts. Blood also soaked his puffy beard as he moved his eyes around, trying to figure out what was happening. His gaze locked onto Erik's, and he looked confused, like he wondered how he could be in this strange situation.

Still staring at Erik, Ketil's mouth spasmed. His face softened and relaxed, and as he slid down the wall, a faint smile crossed his traumatized face. Struck with fear for his comrade, Erik could say nothing else.

Ketil focused on Erik, meeting his gaze with incomprehension and anxiety. Seeing his impending demise, a sense of peace washed over Ketil's face. Gurgling out his final breath, his eyes grew vacant, and he died.

#

Erik crouched over the fallen bull, poking at its blood-caked snout with a small knife. Confused, he raised his eyes to the ceiling as he mulled over the recent attack and what it exactly meant. His mind struggled to take in the events and their bizarre attacker, as well as the loss of yet another close friend.

Looking to the now-missing front door, he noted Kristian standing at the doorway, weapon in hand and prepared for anything else that may attack through it. Nunik was at his side with her spear held out, and the pair looked like they were old friends, people who were always meant to stand together.

Thoughts of a partner for his son briefly warmed his mind, but the need to puzzle through their current situation quickly overwhelmed such a notion. Returning his gaze to the dead animal, Erik pondered over the odd composition of the creature.

Outside, the cloying mist had dissipated, returning to where it had emerged in the darkness of the tree line. No further enemy seemed evident on the surrounding fields, and a calm peace, however temporary, existed in the atmosphere around their brief accommodations.

In the corner, Rand was propped against the wall, where Sigri tended to him faithfully. Awake and apparently not seriously injured, he had a bloody cloth bandage on his arm. Wide-eyed, he inhaled with controlled breaths and stared at the remnants of the battle with a stunned expression.

Near the overturned main table, Galmand sat on a chair, his pained features processing the events. He looked no less shocked than Rand, and his eyes darted from one companion to another.

Standing, Erik put his knife away and faced Galmand. "This animal is…should have been dead. For at least a few days."

"You're not making any sense, Erik," Galmand replied, his voice pleading. "What is dead, cannot live."

"No, Father?" asked Erik. "Its flesh is rancid, like that of the bear that attacked us in the meadow. Its blood does not flow like that of a living thing but is black and thick. How can that be explained?"

Galmand had no rejoinder to this, and he grimaced in silence as he considered Erik's description of their wild-animal aggressor.

From the front of the room, Kristian spoke without turning his head to face the discussion. "What does that mean? Are we being pursued by dead things?"

Erik shook his head and moved his gaze around the rest of the room, taking in the state of the remaining party. Distressed, his eyes fell on the corpse of Ketil before he continued. "I'm not sure, but there must be a way to stop…this from happening."

Putting his hands on his hips, Erik's features became hopeless, and he despaired at the current, seemingly impassable situation. The house became silent, with nobody willing to offer more thoughts about what they all faced.

Standing up from Rand, Sigri moved over to the still body of Ketil. Gesturing to him, she spoke with some conviction, evidently sure of herself. "The devil must control the dead, at least the animals. Is there no end to its evil? How can we prevail against a demon that controls the dead?"

No immediate response came to her revelation, but each of the group turned to look at Ketil at that moment. Worried gazes fell over their deceased friend, as if he too may soon rise to attack his former party.

Taking this as a cue, Galmand rose stiffly and moved over to Ketil. Making the sign of the cross over the corpse, he then reached down and made the same sign in blood on Ketil's forehead. Speaking slowly, he affected a calm voice to the group, having overcome his own despondency after the horrific attack. "'Be strong and courageous; do not be frightened or dismayed, for the Lord your God is with you always.'"

Looking to the doorway and the field beyond, Galmand waved his arm, indicating their distant settlement. "Faith will carry us through these events, friends. Tomorrow, we depart for home, and we will save our people. Somehow."

Glancing around, Erik could see that Kristian, Sigri, Rand, and even Nunik were comforted by Galmand's words, the words of a pastor selling hope to a desperate and dwindling congregation.

Frowning, Erik's own face was less convinced, and breathing deep, he dreaded what the next day had in store for them.

# Chapter Sixteen

On the following day, the survivors of the doomed hunting expedition departed overland for the Eastern Settlement. The weather was cold and brutal as they set out, with a vicious and freezing wind forcing them to lean together as they made their way up and into an interior steppe of the vast island.

Over the next three days, the party made their way through dangerous passes and across fields with ancient animal trails laced throughout. The sky above rarely showed anything more than dark clouds and ominous shadows, forcing a depressing pall on the companions as they made their way slowly south.

Probing ahead, Nunik led the way, using her extensive knowledge of similar geography to find the easiest and least treacherous pathways through rocks and around sheets of ice that had been traveled by few people over the last several thousand years. Behind her came Erik, followed by Galmand, who rode on a donkey taken from an outlying barn on Ungertoq's farm.

Because of his injured leg, Galmand held the reigns of the animal and navigated it well on the various paths, but he was obviously displeased with his status of being disabled for the rest of the party's journey home. Bringing up the end of the column were Kristian, Nunik, Rand, and Sigri, who strode carefully through this unknown region, always wary of the Keelut or the animals they supposed the devil could animate at will.

The reality of travel in Greenland was that it most often took place in the coastal waters, with small boats used in the case of the Norse and canoes by the Inuit. Travelers who tried to move inland over long distances were always taking risks from unsettled ice sheets and frigid areas that offered little respite from the freezing arctic wind that so dominated the windswept icebergs making up ninety percent of the island's surface. Many a hunter on a risky journey had disappeared into the icy inland over the last several centuries, never to be seen again, perhaps leaving their bones to be discovered at some point far in the future.

The reality of the demographic situation was that most of Greenland had been occupied by the Norse before the current wave of Inuit, so it was always difficult to assume who was "native" in that context.

However, it was also the case that the Inuit adapted better to the colder weather patterns descending on the wide geographic area of the arctic north, causing ever-colder subclimates that made the traditional Norse ways of subsisting extremely difficult. Whereas the Inuit continued to expand south with the longer winters, and such patterns reinforced and aided their manner of living, their Norse neighbors had a harder time surviving every year under the increasingly colder climate.

On the third day of moving south toward their home village, the party began descending a long valley that led towards an area the hunters began to recognize. The foliage of the glacier-carved valley moved down in elevation, and in the distance were areas that were used as occasional grazing spaces for herds of goats and sheep, at least when the warmer climate in the past had allowed for it. Additionally, the entire set of lower mountains around them yielded occasional herds of caribou, an animal that was hunted by the Norse to provide ready supplies of meat for their isolated farms and hamlets.

Ahead, the valley descended to a plain, one that held a shallow river, a stream of water that needed to be crossed. As the group trudged toward the cold waters of the icy river, Nunik motioned back to Erik, and with a nod, Erik frowned at the donkey Galmand rode. Apologizing with his eyes to the priest, Erik's intent was clear: the animal would be staying on this side of the river and left to its own ends.

As Galmand grimaced at his traveling predicament and wondered how he would be able to traverse the water, the rest of the party began to undress for the frozen swim across the swift current. Even as Galmand's features grew more worried, the rapidly undressing group, including the injured Rand, teased the cleric with mischievous smiles. Getting down to their long underclothes, they began wadding up their exterior clothes in a ball to carry above themselves when they crossed the flowing stream.

Whether Galmand was to wade his corpulent body into the stream himself or be pulled across the expanse like a towed whale, he wasn't going to come out of this crossing with anything like his dignity.

#

The morning air was frigid, forcing the travelers to lean into their clothing as they tried to keep warm by blowing under their fluffy collars. As the group plodded along the rocky trail, misty condensation plumed from under their cloaks, leaving only their eyes visible as they focused ahead.

The day around them was overcast, but light flooded through the clouds in spots, showing the raw beauty of the undulating terrain from bright rays of sun streaming to the ground in patches. In the distance behind them, the mountainous area was steep and gloomy, while on their path ahead, the scenery grew more flat and pleasant as they plodded forward.

To the front of the striding companions, the trail grew wider and split into two directions. At the point the paths intersected, the area was larger, with one trail leading to the Eastern

Settlement, while the other veered east through a series of frost-laden grassy hills.

The group came to a stop in the more expansive area where the trails met, and each took a moment to withdraw some food and take a break before continuing. As they munched on seeds and jerky, they gazed expectantly down the road to their home village.

Struggling on his crutch, Galmand moved gingerly over to a large boulder that stood near the other direction—away from the trail everyone intended to take. Leaning against the large rock, he took out a handkerchief and wiped his sweating face. He did not look well, and the rigors of the trip were not helping his pallid complexion. The priest also had a sad expression, something that portended more than tiredness or disappointment at the ruinous state of their hunting expedition.

Seeing Galmand's pale face and disturbed features, Erik moved close to him and offered an encouraging mile. "We should be back before tomorrow evening. I hope Thorstein agrees, but either way, we're gettin' on those boats."

Looking down the secondary, less-traveled path, Galmand averted Erik's gaze. "I think you will save the village and our people. I'm counting on it, in fact. You have managed to survive up to this point, which is a testament to your excellent leadership."

Confused, Erik scrunched up his face. "What do ya mean, Father?"

Thinking for a moment, Galmand reached down to the hem of his priestly robe. Pulling it up, he revealed the entirety of his lower injured leg.

Erik gasped at the sight. The wound from the Keelut's claws was impossibly infected. Discolored flesh surrounded the injury, and striated tracks of infection ran under his underclothes farther up the leg. The skin's tone was pale and sickly, even in those areas unaffected by the serious wound.

Leaning to get a closer look at the damaged calf, Erik's speech quickened as he motioned over to his son. "We'll carry you the rest of the way. Good thing that Kristian inherited my sturdy back…"

Smiling sadly, Galmand shook his head as Erik's words faded. Letting the robe drop back, he straightened himself and tried to speak with some authority. "That won't be necessary, Erik; I'm afraid I will not be going with you."

"What are you getting at, Father? You can't go off by yourself."

The rest of the group, responding to Erik's raised and perplexed voice, moved closer to see what was wrong. As they came within earshot, Galmand shook his head, like he was embarrassed because of the developing scene.

"What's the matter?" asked Rand, cocking his head doubtfully.

"The Father is thinking about going towards the ruins instead of back home," replied Erik, pursing his lips in annoyance. "By himself."

"Why would he do that?" asked Kristian, moving to look closer at the priest, like maybe his words would make more sense if he could see the man from but a few feet away.

Galmand kept his voice steady, trying to come across as level-headed as he faced the group's exasperated stares. "Because of my injury. I'm already going to die; it's just a matter of when and how at this point."

Looking suddenly harried and disbelieving, Sigri shook her head vigorously. Stepping closer to Galmand, her tone had a pleading manner, like what he suggested would not only be insane, but it would also eviscerate her understanding of everything that had happened up to this point. "That's not true, Father. We can carry you to the village. My husband will know what to do—he has medicines, and his ships will have a doctor."

Galmand didn't say anything for a moment, merely looking down and focusing on the rocky earth. When he spoke, he sounded at peace, even if a bit afraid. "This wretched creature is after me. Do you expect me to lead it to our village, where it will kill everyone? Just like in the Western Settlement?"

Frustrated, Erik put his hand on Galmand's shoulder. "Father, we aren't animals, we are…friends. We don't leave each other to die just because life isn't convenient."

Smiling, Galmand was touched by Erik's words. Looking to Erik, then the rest, he tried to sound positive. "I have lived a good life, friends. It is rare for a man to live to my age. Think of all the good people like yourselves that God has allowed me to know in my time in this beautiful land. What a blessed life and place it has been, but as must happen with us all, my time is coming to an end."

Kristian looked up at the priest, shaking away his concerned thoughts as he focused on him. "Respectfully, Father, we can't leave you for that…thing. Iqiak said it would come after us anyway."

Nodding, Erik agreed with an exaggerated tone. "Yes, he did. Besides, I couldn't live with myself if I—."

Holding up his arms, Galmand silenced the group with a polite smile. Gesturing to the trail, his voice was kind as he implored his companions. "Are you going to make this old man sit in the middle of this path and cry like an ill-tempered child? Will you drag me screaming back to the settlement? I have to lead the devil away, and you KNOW it will follow me."

There was silence from the group as each of the members took in his inescapable logic. After meeting each of their gazes, they all looked down, avoiding Galmand's softly demanding eyes. It appeared Galmand's sacrifice was to be agreed upon by all, however sad it was.

Except for Erik. Stepping away from Galmand, he began removing his sword from his belt. As the party watched him, he held it out to Kristian.

"Then, I'll go with you, Father. We'll find a way to kill that bastard, together. Afterward, we'll take that rowboat on the river, near the abandoned ruins," Erik said, and he motioned to the rest of the travelers. "We'll meet everyone else in the channel on the ocean—on their boats. There's always a way to survive, we just have to look hard enough to find it."

Still holding out his family's sword, Erik was surprised when Kristian didn't immediately accept it. Instead, Kristian gently pushed it away.

Kristian grinned at his father. "I can do it; you go with everyone else. I'm a better fighter, anyway. It's time for me to do my part. For too long you've been the only one getting things done."

Shaking his head, Erik shoved the weapon farther into his son's hands. He moved his eyes to each of the other party members, telling them with his grave expression it was time to move.

Speaking sternly, Erik motioned them toward the other trail. "No, you won't. You'll take this and protect everyone. You'll get to the settlement and save our people. I can't argue about it, there's no time. You…and everyone here…are the future of what was Greenland. Our descendants may not make this land their home, but at least they'll have a place to call home. Don't make our attempt to save you worthless by being stupid."

Seeing his father's stubbornness and commitment to Galmand, Kristian looked down the long trail to their village.

After glancing at Nunik, as if seeking her input, he nodded his worried approval.

Resigned and sad, Kristian took the sword. Leaning in, he gave his father a sincere hug, then turned away to begin the final leg of the journey home.

Leaving his father and Galmand behind, Kristian moved with halting steps down the earthen path towards their village. Nunik, Rand, and Sigri followed close behind, and all were unsure if they would see the priest or Erik again.

# Chapter Seventeen

The misty afternoon clogged the forest around the warehouse, making visibility difficult amongst the twisting trees and brush. The dense fog made the scenery creepier than was normal, and only the occasional chirp of a bird or a scurrying animal provided evidence anything lived inside the dark canopy of woods.

The besieged warehouse that faced the imposing forest was for the present relatively quiet. The goods, stacked in a continuous defensive line, had been heightened and made more formidable, which had the effect of creating a fortified system similar to a reinforced military defensive barrier.

Facing outward, a host of villagers peered into the gloom of the forbidding woods. Some of them held crossbows, while others leaned against pole weapons as they guarded the perimeter against an as-yet-unseen opponent.

Thorstein walked behind this line of men, staring out with them into the unknown gloom, looking for whatever surely stalked his adopted people. Holding an expensive longsword somewhat awkwardly in his hand, his role of leader of the village had been widened to include being the rallying champion of the hapless defenders.

Behind Thorstein, Baldwin followed along while looking down at a sheet of parchment.

Calling back to Baldwin, Thorstein kept his voice low. "All the farms have been contacted? Nobody remains?"

"Yes, but there were more missing," Baldwin replied, sounding disappointed as he read a list of names of the missing, a list that was fortunately short. "We got everyone out—that was able, anyway."

Stopping, Thorstein asked for the paper with a polite nod of his head. Baldwin gave it to him, and after perusing the column of missing people, Thorstein frowned. "We can only hope they have escaped their residences and will soon join us here."

Baldwin nodded in support of this hope, but he didn't appear optimistic about that possibility. He stayed quiet, waiting for Thorstein's next idea or order. Around them, several children were making gentle noises as they played tag with their mothers.

Thorstein patted Baldwin on the shoulder, making his servant feel hopeful and appreciated, at least for the moment. Their recent days had been a whirlwind of preparations for the colony's survival, and the pressure and fatigue of the endeavor were worn across Baldwin's tired features, making any expression of appreciation from his boss a welcome thing.

Raising his voice, Thorstein called out to the line of defenders, hoping all the people within the defensive positions could hear him. His was not a voice that had in the past inspired people to do great things, but he hoped the evolving events would make his attempt to rally these people worthwhile.

"You are a good people, a people of faith and hard work. I want you to know that I am proud to have called you neighbors, even as we stand together against an enemy that seems to take someone new with each passing day."

Murmurs of agreement greeted this, with nods and approving gazes cast Thorstein's way from many of the villagers.

"Moreover, as we stand on the edge of this precipice, striving to save ourselves and loved ones, I wanted you to know that you have much to be proud of," Thorstein shouted, and he began walking down the line. "You as a people settled the untamed borders of this great land and made it your own. You took the worst that it had to offer and prevailed for hundreds of years. Whatever happens, you can be glad to call yourselves Greenlanders."

The defenders heard Thorstein's exhortations, and they seemed to grow a bit taller from his admiring words. Holding their heads up, some of them smiled, even chancing self-congratulatory grins between one another.

As Thorstein's words died away, though, the calm air grew worried around him. The reality of the moment was this was really all he could say. The villagers were stuck in their spots here without an easy way out, and their already-small numbers of the past had recently been reduced further by some enemy that was stealing their neighbors and leaving bloody trails in their wake.

If this had been some great battle, words of encouragement could be lasting, but with their current situation, the humble residents did not even know who or what they faced. Authority and charisma only go so far to support efforts at survival; going further than that would require something else, something they could grab onto.

Several minutes passed, the momentary happiness of the moment faded, and like so often is the case, the attitudes of the defenders focused on their personal chance to survive. The glory of past generations was one thing, but personal hope in a real future was another.

Frowning, Thorstein could feel the mood change, but he also felt he could do nothing to stop it. Wrinkling his nose, he looked to Baldwin, who appeared equally unsure of what actions would help their joint cause.

From behind, a shout came from the lookout stationed on the roof of the warehouse, a tall man who stood on an elevated point that gave an excellent view of the harbor and the ocean beyond it. "Ships incoming. Ships incoming."

Thorstein turned and quickly made his way up a ladder to join the lookout. As he clambered onto the roof, the villagers below watched him stand high, then extend a crude telescope to peer into the distance. Their eyes and faces were caught in rapt expectation as they awaited the result.

Lowering the visual aid, Thorstein pumped his fist in the air, grinning at the throng of ecstatic and relieved villagers. The crowd broke into raucous applause at their inbound saviors, with wide grins and happy features from all, including workmen, parents, and hopeful children. At last, help had arrived at the end of the known world.

With a grin that spanned his handsome face, Thorstein himself had never in his life been so happy to witness the arrival of his ships. And this time, the reason for his joy had nothing to do with commerce or profit.

#

Around the weak campfire, crumbling stone walls extended into the darkness. Various remnants of the long-ruined walls were strewn over an interior courtyard, and all around the area was the outline of a long-abandoned castle. The crackling flames illuminated the interior dark stones of the walled enclosure, providing the only sound to an old residence that had once housed a powerful and now-forgotten chieftain of the Norse colony.

Though the sky was starry and unhidden by clouds, the walls of the small and dark keep were high enough to obscure most of its penetrating light from filling the dim campsite. This was the intent of its location, to prevent easy detection by the Keelut and to buy Galmand and Erik some time as they hid and tried to rest for the night.

Galmand lay some distance from the insubstantial flames in an alcove, his legs sprawled out before him and covered. Obviously in pain, he grimaced over at Erik, who walked by him and laid some more wood on the fire.

"You have to quit being a hero," said Galmand, gently smiling. "There is a reason such men do not reach old age."

Erik kicked and shuffled some of the kindling together, trying to reach that happy medium of enough warmth from the fire without its light giving away their modest place of refuge. His amused features were just visible in the limited light. "You flatter me, Father. Truth is, I always took the easy way in life, instead of fighting for what's right."

Doubtful, Galmand shook his head. "That's absurd, but I will allow your modesty for now, Erik. At least, as long as you have taken the time to save my old bones from certain death."

Chuckling, Erik pulled his crossbow from his pack. Extending his leg, he held down the weapon and cranked its string into place. Pulling a quarrel from his cloak, he set it into place to make it ready to fire. Moving close to Galmand, he gently laid the missile weapon next to the priest.

"If he should come for us tonight, this will surprise that wretched imp," Erik said. "Try to hit it in the eye, and maybe I can get close enough to cut 'em in half."

Erik patted a backup sword that hung from his waist, one that he had kept in his bag until now. It wasn't as fearsome as his family's special blade, but it would have to do if they were to survive.

Looking carefully down and wrinkling his nose, Erik moved aside Galmand's fur cloak and exposed his injured leg. In the gloomy light, the wound looked even worse, with its jagged edges darkening forebodingly. Frowning at the afflicted limb, Erik moved methodically and changed the simple cloth bandage.

While Erik worked, Galmand nodded thanks and spoke in a low tone. "You were a committed husband to your wife, all the way to the end. Even as consumption wracked her body, you never left her side. You're a godly man."

Surprised by the admiring comments, Erik stopped and looked at his friend. Turning away, he stifled a surge of sadness, like the suggestion of his wife brought her presence closer for the moment. Taking a few breaths to control himself, his voice was somber. "She's in heaven. I don't know nothing about God's earth or heaven, but I know that. I just got to make my way to her; it's been a long wait."

Galmand smiled affectionately, reaching out to pat Erik on the arm as he finished the bandage. "And, God willing, it will be longer still. The village and Kristian still need you."

Done with his medical duty, Erik remained squatting on his haunches. He tried blinking away the sadness that flowed through him, something that always seemed unwelcome and uncontrollable.

Leaning back against the rock wall behind him, Galmand spoke in a reassuring tone. "Blessed are those that mourn, for they shall be comforted."

Erik met Galmand's eyes, which were obscured by the darkness and resembled dark holes in the vague light. Nodding his appreciation, Erik stayed still and considered the priest's words.

Galmand had a way to quote scripture at just the right time, choosing just the right passages to soothe his parishioners' anxious hearts. But, Erik imagined with a nod and a smile, that is why Galmand chose this life—or at least why his religious vocation chose him.

Abruptly from the side, a skittering sound came from the other side of the wall. Looking up, they saw the Keelut climb atop the stone barrier and perch itself there, merely a dozen paces away. Where it stood, the beast's hideous face and form were entirely visible as it peered down. The pale flesh and evil look were just as before, perhaps even made worse by the faint light and its elevated position, like it was a dark angel coming to harvest their iniquitous souls. Looking down at the fire, the creature moved its head around, searching for the two.

It surely must have seen the duo, but it panned its head past them several times, like they were invisible to its wicked eyes. For a long minute, the Keelut crouched still, waiting and watching for them. The companions held their breath, expecting to be quickly attacked by the deadly creature.

As if disappointed, the Keelut seemed to collect itself and scoured the darkness outside of the ruins. With no further action, it clattered down the opposite side of the exterior wall, its claws clicking against the stones as it moved off into the darkness.

The creature had had them at a woeful disadvantage, but neither Galmand nor Erik were attacked. It was as if the wicked devil could not see them and went elsewhere to hunt for the source of the fire in the cold and black night.

With a bewildered look, Erik reached into a pouch of his cloak. Withdrawing the stone that had killed Sigmar, he looked quizzically up to Galmand. Astonished, he rolled the dark stone over in his fingers. As he did so, a faint orange light was visible in its inky black depths. Confused, Erik spoke in a whisper. "It's humming, like it lives."

Concerned, Galmand gestured to the smooth rock. Watching close as its bizarre light faded, he spoke softly. "What could it mean?"

Erik stepped gingerly to the fire, his face a maze of confusion and wonder. He stood there for some time, holding up the stone and pondering what exactly just happened. As he considered their terrible enemy and its pursuit of them, understanding crossed his face.

Turning around, Erik paced close to Galmand and pointed to the priest's crucifix affixed around the cleric's pudgy neck. "It means we have a way to kill it. That is, if you'll let me borrow your cross."

#

Focusing ahead, Kristian breathed deep and stared at the large longhouse. The shutters on its four front windows were left open, and no sound or candlelight emanated from inside its dark interior. Deeply saddened, Kristian turned away from the lonely building and began walking on a rutted pathway toward a series of outbuildings standing on the periphery of the enormous Norse farm. Around him, the fenced fields were empty of livestock or workers.

It was a quiet afternoon, and the air was still, providing a backdrop that matched the deserted feel of the abandoned area. Ahead of him, Kristian's eyes met those of Nunik, who watched him plod her way with a combination of expectancy and dread on her face. When they met gazes, he showed her a deadpan expression, one that turned to sadness as he drew closer.

Walking by Nunik, Kristian nodded at her and proceeded farther up the crude wagon trail. In the distance, at a fork in the path that veered toward the next homestead, stood Rand and Sigri, both of whom waited to see the result of the latest neighbor they had visited this afternoon.

They quickly got the expected bad news from Kristian's scowl and depressed shake of his head. Dropping their heads in defeat, neither knew what to say when Kristian got within earshot.

"Another deserted house," muttered Kristian, not bothering to sound hopeful. "And more blood, like their bodies have been dragged off. We can only hope that at least their kid got away. I knew Olaf since he was born."

Pulling up short of Rand and Sigri, Kristian struggled to get his thoughts around the series of farms they had been visiting all morning. Most were simply empty, but others such as this were filled with splattered blood and the remnants of obvious violence.

Looking up at the cloudy sky, Kristian sighed, hoping that at least somebody remained alive somewhere. *How could he deal with the loss of everyone?*

After a few moments of distressed consideration for his neighbors, Kristian took the family long knife from his belt. Flipping it around, he held it out to Sigri, who peered back with unhidden surprise.

"This is…for what?" asked Sigri, raising an eyebrow.

"It's a peace offering," replied Kristian. "I can't use both swords, and I think only these weapons can hurt that creature. That, or something religious, which we don't have at the moment."

Nodding thankfully, Sigri met Kristian's gaze. "That's kind of you."

Taking the knife, Sigri handed it to her father. Rand took the weapon in his one good hand, holding it out to see how it balanced in his grip. Nodding in appreciation, he met Kristian's gaze with a respectful-if-cool gaze.

Looking at Rand, Sigri gave him a look that said *Get lost, Father.* Frowning, Rand turned around to make himself scarce and walked away to inventory his already-counted supplies elsewhere.

Kristian noticed the abrupt departure and looked inquiringly at his former love. Sigri responded with a defensive expression as she cleared her throat.

"I really wanted to talk some more," said Sigri, glancing over to Nunik to ensure their privacy. "This is difficult to discuss…"

Sigri put her hand on Kristian's arm and left it there. As she met his gaze, her eyes were a mix of confusion and…need, like she wanted something from him. Kristian stared down at her hand, and his expression became tortured and desirous, like this was something he had awaited for a very long time.

Frustration and affection passed from his eyes to hers. They continued their silent interaction for a long pause, both wrestling with feelings that had yet to die away from their youthful infatuation. After some time, Kristian mastered himself, showing a resolve that had been missing in his personality up until now. Taking her hand, he let it drop from his arm.

"Everything we promised and planned for…was all lies," Kristian said, his tone full of despair. "But everything I felt…feel…was all true. You know what that means?"

"I don't understand."

"It means you were my undying love," continued Kristian. "I would have died for you—in a second, without question. But for you, I was 'good enough' until your rich husband wanted a young and pretty wife."

Sigri scowled, shaking her head. "It isn't like that."

"Yes, it is. Doesn't really make sense to lie about it now," responded Kristian, and he huffed in annoyance. "But I guess this is life. Just because one person feels one way, it doesn't mean the other has to."

Sigri raised her voice, mixing her notion of compassion for Kristian with a pleading tone. "Can't you just look at it my way?"

"No need now, Sigri, I get it. And I won't be your enemy—or your husband's. I actually wish you both well."

Kristian clearly didn't mean that, and his face was a mask of contrasting emotions as he mulled over their situation. Even in this distant corner of the world, love and hate always lay in close proximity to one another, and Kristian now felt both emotions in surging abundance.

Sigri nodded, but she didn't appear completely happy. "We can still be friends…"

"I'm not your friend—and never will be. I just get that I gotta get past this. A person can only be stupid for so long."

"You're being unfair," replied Sigri, letting hurt move into her features.

Kristian shook his head, frustrated and in far more emotional pain. "At least be who you are, Sigri. You can't have both the young boyfriend's attention and the rich old husband—

it doesn't work that way, even a stupid young man can see that. You're no longer mine to be concerned about; you've made sure of that. Now, it's Thorstein's turn to get used."

Dropping his eyes from Sigri, Kristian turned and paced slowly away from her. His jaw quivered as he moved toward the next farm, and he kept his eyes fixed on the open terrain of brush and pastures straight ahead—anything to avoid looking back.

As Nunik moved to join him, Kristian's steps grew quicker. Trudging ahead, they picked up the pace, padding across the muddy path of the less-traveled countryside. Arching her neck, Nunik glanced back at Sigri, showing a look of disdain that was easily understood in either of their cultures.

Looking on from the side, Rand watched Kristian and Nunik continue the journey toward the inner farms of the village. Grimacing, he rolled his eyes at the whole spectacle.

# Chapter Eighteen

The glow of the sun washed across the broken wall of the old castle grounds. In the daylight, the area was less foreboding, with the scattered stones of the crumbling building piled in heaps amongst shrubbery and undergrowth. The effect of the abandoned keep and the nearby vegetation was a lonely one. The remnants of the former habitation had fallen away, and it now appeared that nature and the frigid tundra were to reclaim their former hold over the place.

On the outside of the wall was a campfire, placed near a row of dark rocks and in view of the entire area around the modestly sited castle. Galmand sat reclined against the ordered stones, warming himself near the flames and looking distressed as he brooded in solitude.

Galmand's face was sweaty and feverish in the crisp afternoon breeze, and his eyes flitted nervously around as he tugged at his substantial beard. His was not the face of one who was comfortable with his environment but was instead full of anguish and worry.

Opposite Galmand from the tree line, only fifty yards away, the Keelut emerged. With a shimmer, the camouflaged outline of the creature dropped away, and its striated whitish-gray flesh became visible. Stepping from the cover of the woods, it fixed its dark eyes on the apparently defenseless priest.

Creeping forward, the beast's soulless eyes focused entirely on Galmand. The waiting cleric met the gaze of the monster's otherworldly stare, and his mind recoiled in fear and horrible dread at what he witnessed: the reality of an insidious demon, one who was coming to take him for its malevolent purpose.

As if to acknowledge its upcoming victory and perhaps a meal, the pupil-less eyes grew almost animated, as if the creature was certain of its success. Galmand shivered as its clawed feet stepped closer to him.

Casting aside the cloak that covered his legs, Galmand held up a large silver cross, one that he had brought on this expedition within his personal possessions. Meant to be used for religious processions, its size was substantial and heavy, like that of a blunt weapon. Galmand held up the cross defensively, and his hands were clad in the thick leather gloves Erik had bought from the vendor at the market in the Eastern Settlement. The old hard leather and crusader's cross of the protective coverings were visible on both hands.

Surprised, the Keelut was immediately wary of Galmand. The creature still advanced toward him, but it moved to one side, as if seeking an angle of attack that offered a way to avoid the cross. Getting close to him, it crouched to one side, and its lithe legs, coiled in grotesque muscles, were ready to leap.

Boldly holding up the cross, Galmand shuffled his weight to the side and tried to face the incoming threat, his determined features steeling in anticipation for what came next. He was not a person made for physical confrontation, but his eyes told the story of a man who accepted what must be done, no matter the result. Hardening his jaw, Galmand met the being's evil stare without reservation, knowing his end could be near.

The Keelut sprang ahead, raking its razor-black claws forward. Grasping the metal of the large crucifix, an immediate hissing and wisp of smoke met its touch. The other attacking claws scraped across Galmand's hard leather gloves, with no noticeable result on their surface. Leaping backward, the beast pulled back its limbs and wailed in pain, for the moment unsure how to next attack its formerly vulnerable prey.

As if indecisive, the creature scanned the area, visibly looking for another avenue of aggression. As it did so, Erik stepped gingerly from an area behind it, from a place of piled brush that had hidden him up to this point. Emerging from shrubbery stacked to camouflage his own presence, Erik was only a short distance behind the beast. Stepping carefully, he moved quietly and focused ahead.

Kneeling cautiously, Erik aimed down the crossbow and released the trigger mechanism. The quarrel projectile flew straight, striking the Keelut precisely in the back. At the end of the bolt was the sharp edge of Galmand's small cross, fashioned by Erik into an approximation of a barbed missile. It plunged deep within the torso of the Keelut, piercing its insides acutely.

The beast screamed and flung itself to the side, reaching back and trying to get at the burning barb that skewered it so deeply. The wails of the demonic being were otherworldly and frantic, and the pain evident in its cries was as if from another place, like they came from hell itself.

Rushing forward, Erik drew out his sword and closed on the creature. Raising his weapon high, he brought it down in an attempt to finish its wretched existence, to cleave deep within its putrid flesh.

Insanely fast, the Keelut spun and grabbed the blade, as if the devil felt his approach. The edge of the sword cut into its hand as it held off Erik's attack. Its dark eyes stared wickedly up at Erik, even as the hissing and burning of the bolt within it caused the beast to mewl in agonizing pain.

Pushing itself upright, the Keelut's strength was formidable. It forced Erik back and twisted his sword arm until the blade was forced down toward Erik's own panicked eyes. Forced to one knee, Erik grabbed the other end of the blade, cutting his hand with his own weapon to keep his head from being sliced open with the edge. The creature's expression, though not capable of emotions as a human would know it, seemed to grin at Erik's upcoming demise.

With a rush, Galmand's substantial frame ran into the beast, knocking it to the ground. Suddenly able to move around, the priest raised his cross and struck the Keelut, bashing its skull with the large crucifix. Over and over, he used the implement to brain the demon, and each strike of the cross caused yet more shrieks, hissing, and wails from the grievously wounded creature.

Joining Galmand, Erik raised his own weapon and thrust it into the prostrated creature, ramming the sharp end of his blade into its torso, head, and legs. As the screams of the beast died down, Erik used the cutting edge of the sword to cleave into its hideous body. With a final thunk, he severed the abominable head of the Keelut, and its horrible sounds stopped abruptly.

Stopping their attacks, Erik and Galmand looked at one another, Erik with his gore-splattered blade and Galmand with his now-misshapen cross. Black blood from their now-vanquished enemy covered their bodies, like they had themselves been dipped in the detritus of their foe.

For some time after, they stood there, seemingly surprised by their own success. Galmand, who for a time had overcome his leg wound to stand and fight, grinned at Erik under the splashed residue of their demonic opponent. Each wore the face of a warrior that had fought the good fight—and won.

#

Night was descending over the warehouse, shrouding the area in elongated and obscuring shadows. Only a few rays of light from the west remained, coloring the large building with a final orange hue. No sounds or lights were evident, and only splashing from nearby waves on the shoreline offered respite from the silence of the abandoned area.

Deserted, a strange calm lay over the former commerce site. Where men had bustled and toiled at the task of trade for hundreds of years was now replaced by stacks of yet-to-be loaded goods and abandoned personal items. Things that would have made men rich were now merely discarded and unimportant.

Kristian walked among the barricades in front of the warehouse, his features a mix of confusion and anxiety. He pointed to the rows of crates and clutter, frowning at the ensemble of worldly things. "It looks like they took all the food, That's a good sign, right?"

With a worried cant of her head, Nunik stopped at a wooden crate filled with valuable rope fashioned from the hides of walrus. She ran her hand over the outside, nodding at the confines of the open-sided crate. "If they leave such important things, will they come back? I thought they were family? Family never leave each other, no?"

From the side, a slam of a door, and Sigri paced from the warehouse entrance. Her face was agitated and unhappy as she raised her voice. "He took all his papers and books. He wouldn't leave me."

Sigri's disappointment and concern indicated she wasn't completely sure of that statement. She stopped and searched the area around herself, as if Thorstein might pop out from behind his valuable commodities. Taking several deep breaths, she ran her hands through her hair, processing what this scene of abandonment could mean on both a personal and collective level.

Walking up to his daughter, Rand moved to comfort Sigri, a look of genuine concern filling his face. Using his one good arm, he offered her an awkward hug. She returned the gesture with an appreciative nod.

"Look," shouted Nunik, pointing to the forest.

At the entrance to the canopy of woods, the familiar and dreaded fog appeared, collecting and growing dense amongst the brush and trees. Soon, a bank of the mist was evident, percolating with an insistent roil within the darkness of the gloomy foliage. For several moments, the party traded startled glances with each other, knowing the unnatural fog portended the return of their unnatural enemy.

Grabbing Nunik's arm, Kristian pointed to the shoreline, towards an area some distance from the developing mist. He tried to keep a calm voice, but his words and demeanor were alarmed. "Let's get down to the shoreline. We'll go east."

#

Squishing among the mud and shallow water, the group hiked through the waves of the mild surf. Kristian was in the lead, his eyes scouring the impending darkness and the mist along the tree line to his left. He held a torch in his hand, but the dwindling light from its almost-burned-out form made the flames seem insignificant as his gaze probed ahead.

Behind him, Nunik, Rand, and Sigri followed, their eyes also searching their dank surroundings. The entirety of the party had the rushed and panicked appearance of prey, lost in the moonless night and trying to come to terms with diminishing prospects for a way out of their encroaching hell.

Out to sea, a gentle mist, one that was entirely normal and did not glow with the threat of their otherworldly attacker, hung over the lapping waves of the ocean. Combined with the oncoming darkness of night, visibility over the water was limited to a few yards. The perceivable world of the companions was reduced to a scant few paces as they scoured their near environment, and they sloshed onward with trepidation as they sought to keep their footing in the frigid surf.

Trying to catch her breath, Sigri tried to support her father as she called forward. "Slow down, we can't keep up."

Glancing back, Kristian nodded but only slowed somewhat. Striding onward, he picked his way over the slippery rocks, keeping his focus on staying ahead of their enemy. His bearing was brave, but his flitting eyes revealed the face of one who was all too aware their time was running out.

It seemed to Kristian that this whole event was woefully unfair, with all of their efforts and trials seeming to come to an end too soon, without a definable reason or sense of purpose. They as a group and a people had endured so much, trying to survive against all odds while also being true to their culture and faith. What was it all for, if they were only to be extinguished by this unknowable evil that had hounded them across this vast island?

But his father had been right about that all along, Kristian supposed. Life was unfair, pure and simple, with faithful and God-fearing folk always seeming to bear the brunt of the worst the world could offer. He had heard from someone in the village that in the recent past, whole cities of people had been killed by plagues, or a "black death," throughout much of the rest of the European world.

Though such an illness had never affected their home here, it was apparent from its existence that misfortune came to call on man everywhere, and maybe it was now time that their own end was at hand. Bad stories of war and death had always seemed to affect others, but the reality was, there came a time when suffering could also visit their own lives in a very real way.

Ahead, a dark man-sized silhouette revealed itself on the shoreline, its features undefined in the dim background of the gathering night and fog. The figure was stopped and appeared to focus on them, as if unsure what exactly the party was in the shallow ocean waters.

Holding out his long blade, Kristian pointed the sword at the form, also unsure of who or what he faced. To his side, Nunik, Sigri, and Rand strode up next to him, also coming to a halt. Each held out their own weapon, their eyes searching before them as the unknown figure returned their desperate gazes.

Haggard and unsure, the four remaining hunters focused for some time, preparing for what could come next: their last stand in the cold shallows of lonely waters in the Greenland Sea.

# Chapter Nineteen

The normal visual occurrence of oppressive mist and overcast sky was missing in the isolated area near the crumbled remains of the castle. Birds chirped near the camp area where Galmand and Erik had made their stand against their horrid pursuer, and the air was for the moment clear of the biting cold that so often soaked the life from this barren area.

Near the castle, morning light illuminated the area around a small river, providing an unusually bright and pleasant enhancement to distant mountain ranges populated by ridges of clear and shining glaciers.

On a bluff above the placid water of the small river stood Erik and Galmand. Momentarily quiet, they took turns looking at each other and then out over the untamed area that surrounded them. Caught up in personal thoughts of what this meant for their former lives, each was unwilling to broach the subject of their upcoming attempt to flee their homeland.

Truth was, not only was their fight against the Keelut an existential one, but their whole time coming to a final close on this continent-sized island made for a particularly sorrowful feeling. Galmand himself was descended from the initial settlers that settled here in the late 900s, which was something that made fleeing the area seem like a betrayal to his ancestors. They had struggled and persevered, eventually even setting up settlements far to the west—in a region of the world unknown even to other Europeans.

Now, it was all going to be over, and who was to know if their lives had ever even happened here? Who would sing their praises or know of these hardy people, those that had done so much with so little? Even for a man like Galmand, a person whose whole life was spent serving God and the afterlife, is just seemed so sad and useless. Civilization was something pursued to extend the life of a culture, not to die out under the cold and hooves of some otherworldly force.

On the river near a bend in the gentle current was a rowboat tied to a wilted tree. Used for fishing or to facilitate the crossing of the flowing water, it was left for whomever needed it in the day-to-day way of life for the Norse. That it was now the last way to escape their home was an ironic expression of the usefulness of that gesture of communal ownership.

Grimacing, Erik touched the surface wound on his hand that he received in the struggle with the Keelut. Straightening his grimy tunic, he held up the black stone with his other hand.

"Somehow, this hid us from that devil. Wish we'd known that sooner."

Galmand replied with a grin, merely nodding as he took in the odd stone and its effect on their chances for survival. The priest's color had returned to his face, and for the moment, the infection from his leg wound seemed to have subsided.

Reaching down, Erik lifted and shouldered his leather pack. Tucking away the strange smooth rock, he allowed a measure of contentment to enter his hopeful tone. "We make quite a team, a broken-down farmer and an aging priest."

Galmand nodded and grinned. "That we do. An unlikely pair to confront the devil at the end of the world."

Gesturing down to the boat, Erik patted Galmand on the shoulder. "Rest yourself, Father. I'll get the boat ready, and we'll find that rich bastard, Thorstein, to take us out of here. If not, I'll row us to Iceland myself."

Erik grinned to show he was only half-joking about rowing across the ocean if needed. Galmand frowned at Erik's sentiment and language as he descended the hill to the river. For all his good qualities, Erik could be crotchety and unforgiving when he felt the need.

Galmand sighed as he realized he would have time to improve on the concept of forgiveness with Erik, both because of his past with Thorstein and to ensure Erik's own son didn't fall into the trap of thinking forgiveness showed weakness. The work of a priest was never done, it seemed, and Galmand beamed with inner contentment at still being needed by his flock.

At the river, Erik loaded his limited supplies into the boat. Checking the exterior of the craft for water-worthiness, he pushed it mildly into the current, visually inspecting it for proper buoyancy. Happy with what he saw, Erik turned to get Galmand's attention above him.

His eyes locked in terror at what he saw.

Atop the bluff, three Keeluts surrounded Galmand, one of which had a missing clawed hand from its earlier encounter with Erik. Focusing on the priest, they advanced on the horrified cleric, who stumbled as he spun around in panic.

Grabbing at his waist, Erik prepared to draw his sword, but just then, Galmand met his eyes from his hopeless position above him. The priest shook his head, indicating what both of them knew: if Erik rushed to help, they would both be killed.

With a rush, the monsters swarmed over Galmand. Quickly subduing him, they slowly disemboweled the portly man, tearing out his guts while the horrified cleric screamed in unrestrained fear and agony. It took some time for the priest's wails to stop, and much of his insides were yanked free from his torso before he was finally silent.

Disbelieving what he was witnessing, Erik had watched the creatures kill his friend without mercy, unable to even make a sound to help him as he hid under the virtual cloak of the black rock. With each mortal wound they had inflicted on Galmand, Erik's helpless eyes had grown more distant and unseeing.

When Galmand's mouth had locked open and his death stare faced the sky, the beasts collected his guts in strings around their putrid white and gray bodies, slinging the intestines and organs over their shoulders as if preparing for a journey.

Dragging his corpse to the edge of the bluff, the Keeluts threw his body into the water with a sickly splash. Moving away from the hill, the creatures disappeared into the cover of brush that ran down the side of the ridge opposite the river.

When the devils were gone, the silent and shocked Erik, still standing near the rowboat, watched his dead friend float by. As tears streamed down Erik's face, Galmand's corpse gently rolled over in the current, as if at that moment Galmand couldn't bear for Erik to see him in that condition.

#

The roiling waves of the open ocean were high but not extreme. In the distance could be heard the shrieks of seagulls, indicating that land was not far off. The mostly blue sky above was filled with a chilly wind, but the day could be considered mild by any arctic designation.

Erik sat in the rowboat, his eyes focused on endless whitecaps that rolled into the foamy distance. He was there in mind, but his spirit looked to be missing. He watched without seeing, experiencing the pull of the waves and the movement of the oars across the surface without really registering his surroundings. The bobbing of the simple craft continued for several minutes, and over time, it appeared Erik was not particularly concerned with his destination, such was his sorrow over Galmand's death.

The distant call of "ship!" reached Erik's ears, and he moved his head to take in a site on the periphery of the horizon. Two cargo ships, so-called knarrs, had come within earshot and were making their way under sail toward Erik's small boat. As they moved closer, Erik perked up, tilting his head in curiosity.

Pulling alongside his erstwhile escape craft, a line was cast down from the leading cargo vessel. Moving without much motivation, Erik used it to scale the side of the knarr until he reached the rigging. From there, he climbed up towards the railing, moving slowly to ensure his safety.

Clambering the last few yards, a host of villagers from the Eastern Settlement came into Erik's view. As he looked farther down the railing, he saw his son smiling at him, and Erik came out of his stupor to return a joyful smile at Kristian. Next to Kristian was Nunik, who looked like she was made to stand at the side of his much-taller son. Even on the crowded railing, they leaned closer than needed, contented for the moment with the proximity of each other's company.

Closer to where Erik ascended was Sigri, and her eyes shone with happiness at seeing him, even as she moved her gaze to the empty rowboat behind him. Her pleasant grin faded as she took in what that could only mean.

Getting near the top, Thorstein stuck his head over to look down at him. The merchant raised his eyebrows to inquire about Galmand, but a pained shake of Erik's head was the only response forthcoming.

When Erik managed his way to the top, Thorstein's expression went from a frown at the distressing news of the priest to a genuine moment of satisfaction at seeing his former enemy alive. Reaching out, he took Erik's hand and helped him aboard with a hearty and long-missing smile.

At that, the remnants of the Eastern Settlement, the last Norse people to make their home in Greenland, looked as one towards the eastern skyline. The two cargo ships, with experienced crews performing all the requisite duties, worked the rigging to come about and return to Iceland.

# Chapter Twenty

## Nuuk, Greenland - Present Day

Sunlight flooded into the hotel room, casting patches of the summer's bright rays across the interior of the simple room. On a table in the middle of a kitchenette area was a collection of beer and liquor, with some bottles half-full and others long since drained of their important liquid.

At the far end of the room was a large bed, and in its middle slumbered a stretched-out and contorted woman. Wrapped in sheets and mismatched blankets, Lisbeth snored loudly. In her middle thirties and thin, her back was arched as she labored through several inebriated exhalations. Looking the worse for wear, she had the appearance of being run over by a liquor truck, and matched with her deep sleep, she looked capable of passing the entire day in this self-induced condition.

On the pillow next to her head, a hard-rock ringtone announced an incoming call. Stopping her snoring, Lisbeth reached to her phone and numbly pulled it next to her still-closed eyes.

"Yeah?" answered Lisbeth, speaking in Danish. She smacked her lips several times, apparently unhappy with the taste in her mouth. "Oh shit, not already?"

Her eyes popping open, Lisbeth moved them around to focus on the rest of the room. With everything coming into focus, some panic found its way into her voice. "Sorry, I'll be down in a minute. Tell them I was sick—morning sickness or something."

Throwing the phone on her covers, Lisbeth stumbled from the bed and angled toward the bathroom. Bumping into the wall on several occasions, she finally found her way inside the tight-quartered area.

Clicking on the light, she looked shocked at her own appearance in the mirror, taking some time to peer at her pale white skin in the flickering bathroom light. After trying to make herself presentable by ruffling her bed-head hairdo with her fingers, she gave up and grimaced at the hungover image.

Lifting her right arm, she sniffed her underarm and rewarded herself with a disgusted look from the resulting odor. Pursing her lips, she shook her head and opened and closed her bloodshot eyes several times, trying to acclimate herself to the reality of the new day.

"Well, get moving, you drunken bitch," said Lisbeth, in what passed for self-motivation. Sighing, she reached over and turned on the shower with a WHOOSH.

#

Striding into the lobby, Lisbeth looked much better. Having transformed herself with a shower and some makeup, she was the image of a professional and attractive woman. Her dark hair was tied in a ponytail, and glasses were now perched on her nose, evincing a knowledgeable and intelligent expression.

The lobby around her was tidy, with a TV in the background playing a droning sportscaster of some sport or other.

As Lisbeth glanced around, Hans stared at her from over a newspaper in a lobby chair. Younger than Lisbeth by a few years, his perfectly trimmed goatee had the opposite effect than what he wanted; it somehow made him look younger.

Standing, Hans offered her a knowing smile. "Nice of you to join the living. I thought you drank all the available wine in Greenland."

Returning his look with a fake smile, Lisbeth motioned out the door. "Very funny. I noticed you closed down the bar—and somehow found a way for me to pay the outrageous tab. What happened to male chivalry?"

"It went out with my last car payment. Besides, I can't remember what time I flew in yesterday, much less what happened last night."

Grinning and pointing to the side, Hans took the lead and walked toward a restaurant that abutted the main lobby. As he entered the establishment, he passed a sign that read "Welcome Hvalsey Archaeology Attendees."

Frowning, Lisbeth followed him into the dimly lit eatery, which looked a bit like a cross between a coffee shop and a street coffee vendor. Walking toward the back of the place, she passed a TV that was playing the news.

Sliding into a booth across from Hans, she noticed he was already buttering up a large muffin. Eagerly finishing the preparation, he left a large glob of unmelted butter on the bread. As he wolfed it down, crumbs fell around the area, where two more plates contained sliced boiled eggs and assorted crackers with jelly.

Finishing up his breakfast, Hans gulped down a foamy glass of milk and motioned for Lisbeth to dig into the assorted food. She politely declined, raising a lip in disgust and pushing the plates to the side.

"Most everyone went last night," said Hans, gesturing out the window at the wider world. "They wanted to get an early start. But, Brad and Liam should be here soon, said they'd let you recover a bit before diving into work."

Grinning, Hans then held up his newspaper, showing her a proud smile. "And, you're famous, or at least should be soon."

In the Danish newspaper was the headline *Mystery Finally Solved?* Below the headline was a poor photo of an archaeological dig in a large cave system.

Tapping the newspaper, Hans lowered his voice, as if he was dealing with top-secret material. "How sure are you of your conclusions?"

Shrugging, Lisbeth tried to keep her voice normal, but she still came across as defensive. "As much as I can be. They've been trying to figure this out for almost three hundred years, since the Danes returned to re-colonize the island: what happened to the Norse in Greenland?"

Hans continued in his conspiracy-themed low voice. "The rest of the conference thinks it's climate change, or Inuit warfare, or maybe habitat destruction by their farming methods. Some even think Basque whaler raids. Or, maybe it's some combination of those things. Why the difference with you?"

Chewing on her lip, Lisbeth shook her head. "These skeletons we're finding are showing signs of cannibalism. Stored in caves where nobody lived? What else could cause that?"

Exasperated, Hans rolled his eyes. "Medieval cannibals? Some kind of unknown animal? How could that account for driving people out of a country where they'd lived for hundreds of years? It sounds like a fairy tale—and the end of your quest for tenure."

"Just wait until you've seen my evidence, that's all I ask. Just have an open mind. The world is full of mysteries…"

Hans' formerly lively expression changed to something else, and he suddenly looked like a scared child. Staring at the TV behind Lisbeth, his terrified eyes were locked open. Standing slowly, he moved to the elevated screen and raised the volume on the TV manually, while Lisbeth spun around to see what was going on.

On the screen, there was police tape stretched across a cave entrance. To the side, there were several archaeological tents used for processing digs and allowing for assistants to live and work onsite. Next to the tents was a sign, *The Hvalsey Project*, and the TV screen showed "Live" in the corner of the video image.

Two medical workers carried a body out of the cave, with the shape of a victim below a bloodstained white sheet. Several policemen stood around the scene, looking confused and overwhelmed by whatever had happened.

The newscaster's voice broke through the background. "…multiple bodies have been recovered, and police have no motive for the massacre at the archaeological site. Further investigations will continue as the authorities come to terms with the scale of the murders. Outlying communities are being warned to lock their doors…"

As the horrific broadcast continued, a dense fog began to swirl across the camera's view, blocking the visibility of the crime scene. The mist began to churn unnaturally, and the police and medical personnel on the broadcast were lost from view.

Startled, Hans and Lisbeth looked at each other, then back again to the TV.

Screams and agonizing shrieks emerged from the seething fog.

# The End

# About the Author

Tim lives in Nevada, where he makes a life enjoying all things horror and thriller-related, from films to books, and even the occasional convention. He has three children, three cats, and he enjoys providing reading entertainment for the monster and creature-loving masses.

**If you like this novel, he would appreciate a review or a follow on Facebook:**

https://www.facebook.com/Horrorthrillerguy

https://www.amazon.com/Timothy-Bryan/e/B09FTFHT5B

https://www.horrorthrillerguy.com

For the opportunity to win free hardcover versions of this and all future books, please join his mailing list:
https://mailchi.mp/143ae89c5418/horrorthrillerguy

**Also by Timothy Bryan:**

*Chindi*

https://www.amazon.com/dp/B09FSCS87K

*The Huntsman of Corvinus*

https://www.amazon.com/dp/B09J8R5XFJ

*Despicable*

https://www.amazon.com/dp/B09SHBX3HS

Printed in Great Britain
by Amazon

18719525R00169